# THE DAY OF THE DOOR

# THE DAY OF THE DOOR

## LAUREL HIGHTOWER

**Ghoulish Books**
San Antonio, Texas

**The Day of the Door**
Copyright © 2024 Laurel Hightower

ISBN: 978-1-943720-96-5

www.Ghoulish.rip

Cover by Trevor Henderson

## Also by Laurel Hightower

*For Sebastian, because everything I have belongs to you.*

# "PLEASE DON'T TAKE HIM."

Every ounce of sixteen-year-old Nathan Lasco's will, every trickle of strength he possessed went into those four words. The *please* hurt the most, his fury and pride a jagged stone in his throat, but fear made him swallow it down. Hot tears burning tracks along his stinging cheeks, he kept his eyes focused and clear by force of will. Everything in his world depended on this, on his ability to keep his brother in sight. It was only by this tenuous connection he could keep Shawn alive. Once it was cut, he'd be lost forever. Nate didn't know how he knew this, but he didn't question it. Whatever childhood trust might have still flickered in his heart had snuffed out with the crack of metal on bone. There was no safety net, and never had been. It was life or death.

Shawn's gaze didn't waver from the woman holding the bat, his teeth bared, blood joining the sweat and tears lining his young face. His will was focused only on her, on changing the game, making her pay. He was too angry for anything else, and the lines already crossed that day weren't ones that could ever be taken back. They'd all felt the tremors of it, even Katy, the youngest—this day would forever mark a *before* and *after*. Nate silently asked for it to stop, begged whatever invisible being might be in the sky—or unseen angels hovering nearby—to stop things here, not let them go any further. There'd never been an answer before, but surely this time, this day, with lives at stake, someone would intervene.

Glassy, empty eyes stared back at him above a twisted snarl of a mouth. There was nothing in those eyes, no understanding of what she'd done, no remorse. Her chin trembled with the force of her fury, her jaw clenched tight. For the space of several heartbeats she didn't answer, and

Nate had time to hope there was still someone in there, a consciousness capable of reason, of empathy. His sisters clung close to him as silently as they could, no one moving as hope spun out to a shining filament.

The thread snapped when she turned her back on them, grabbed Shawn by the shoulder and shoved him stumbling forward. Nate winced, knowing what that little added indignity would do to Shawn, that it might be enough to crack his tight control.

"Move, you little bastard," she bit out, her voice inhuman in its cruelty. When Shawn fumbled at the door she pushed him again, this time with enough force to bang him into the frame. He faced her, one hand fumbling in his pocket, but she marched past him. Turning, she waited just within the room, two steps over the threshold. Shawn stood tall before her, his shoulders shaking, gripping something in his right hand.

When he didn't follow her, she leaned close. "Get in here, *now*."

"Shawn," said Nate, his voice catching. Fear had swallowed every trace of anger, and he reached out. "Don't," he said when his brother looked back at him.

Shawn stood with his chin trembling, his lanky body shaking. Whether from fear or fury, Nate didn't know, and in that stretched moment, he believed they could still turn from this path. That for once Shawn might defy Stella's orders, walk away from her goading. They could leave together, all four of them. Walk out the front door and never look back. Even living on the street would be better than this hell, and Nate could almost see that future unspooling before him.

Stella's cold, inhuman voice dispelled the fantasy. "Don't make me come collect you, Shawn Lasco. It'll be worse if you do."

*Worse?* Nate wanted to scream. How could it get worse than this, right now? They trembled on the precipice of loss, and he knew Shawn felt it, too. But instead of turning his back on Stella and joining his siblings, Shawn nodded once to Nate, gave a sickly smile, and marched to his fate. That path of safety closed for good, leaving only one ending.

Stella's eyes sparked an impossible blue, and she smiled in sick triumph. Nate launched himself at her, but she slammed the door in his face, and Shawn was lost to him forever.

Behind the door. Dark grain wood, solid core, it stood between the three and their brother. Thick as it was, it only halfway muffled the shrieks, screams, curses and thuds that came from the other side while they beat their fists against it, their tears absorbed by that unforgiving surface. Nate lost track of time, it had no meaning while he and his sisters howled and begged, kicked and knocked and clawed at its impassive face. It wasn't until he'd slid down it, sobbing and spent, his fingers and knuckles bleeding, bare feet bruised and aching, that he realized the sounds of struggle had fallen silent behind the door.

That was the real moment hope died in Nate's heart. For he knew the silence didn't mean a spent force, an altercation finished with both opponents licking their wounds. That wasn't how things worked in the Lasco household, and so when his eldest sister brought him the phone, when she dialed for help when he couldn't make himself get off the floor, hope did not return. Slumped with his face pressed tight against the harsh wood, Nate felt for the first time that pain, that severing, the *never again* that he knew awaited them on the other side.

And when that door opened, when it was forced by strange hands, and the children came to the raw knowledge that their quartet had become a trio, the only other person on that side of the door, the only one who made it through alive, was Stella. And if there was one thing these three had learned in their young lives, a lesson imparted alongside the member they lost, it was that their mother could never be trusted.

# CHAPTER ONE

"**I**T WASN'T A fucking haunting." Nate Lasco regretted his use of the curse, the tightness of his voice and chest. He breathed in slow, let it out slower, and promised himself he'd do better.

"That's not what she's saying. Not exactly, anyway—that's the point, no one knows for sure." His youngest sister's voice was bright, still filled with unjustified hope as she pleaded with him. He'd never understood that hope—she should know better by now.

"That's right," he said, calmer. "No one knows for sure, but I can tell you what it wasn't—whatever supernatural bullshit she's trying to feed you now. You know better than this, Katy. She won't ever get better until she accepts responsibility, and she'll never do that. Don't get sucked in, not again."

His youngest sister sighed, a breathy wheeze to it that piqued his concern. Her asthma was acting up , and no wonder. Allergens and everything else affected it, but so did stress. Specifically, family stress—whenever things got bad, Katy's lungs closed up, her breathing a tight whistle until it sealed off altogether. A vulnerability their mother gleefully exploited when given the chance, at the same time she dismissed it as a ploy for attention. The sound of Katy's labored breath made him uneasy in ways he didn't understand, except that he damn well didn't want to lose another sibling.

"Are you using your inhaler?" he asked before he could

4

stop himself. He squeezed his eyes shut against yet another failure. He wasn't responsible for his sisters, for any of his family, and they didn't need him to be. He had to stop trying to be someone he wasn't. Maybe another twenty years and he'd finally get there.

She didn't get pissed, though, not like Aury would have. She gave a short, tinkling laugh. "Always looking out for me. I appreciate that, big bro, but I'm a grown-up now. I don't need your supervision anymore."

"No, you need something else from me."

Katy clucked her tongue. "Not for me, for Mom."

"Stella," he said, jaw clenching.

"She's our mother, Nate. Calling her something else won't change that."

"Neither will giving in to her latest whim. Don't you remember how many times she's done this? She gets us all stirred up, for nothing but another delusion. There were no ghosts."

Her voice was small when she answered. "You know that's not true. We were all there—we all saw—"

"We saw what she wanted us to. We were kids, Katy, kids who were scared shitless, with good reason. But no fucking ghost killed our brother."

"I'm not saying it did. I know . . . I realize Mom bears some responsibility—"

"*Some?*"

"—but what if it wasn't just her? And what if we can help her? I mean, *really* help her."

Nate struggled with his temper. "I'm not going down this road with you. It only enables her, but really? Even if you told me doing this would cure her, make her whole and normal and totally rational again, I wouldn't do it." Anger bled through his tone again but he didn't bother backtracking.

"Because of Shawn," she said softly.

He closed his eyes. "Of course because of Shawn. There's no fucking statute of limitations on murder."

"She said—"

He gritted his teeth. "That it was an accident. I know. I've heard the same bullshit story as you, but I'm not that naive."

Her voice tightened. "So now I'm naive?"

He sighed, pulled back on his frustration. "I can't keep circling back to this. We're never going to know."

"That's just it," she said, her voice so low he had to strain to catch it. "She says she's going to tell us. All of it."

Nate's breath caught, his face going cold. "About Shawn?" he asked, his own voice sounding far away. "Bullshit."

"It's not. She says she's started remembering things—stuff she'd blocked out before."

"What stuff?" asked Nate, suspicion heavy in his tone.

"About the house. About what happened to us there, all of us. That's a big part of why she wants to do this—to get everything out in the open, answer our questions. Put it to rest." She paused, a heavy shadow looming over those two beats of silence. "Put *him* to rest."

Tears burned his eyes, threatening to spill over, but he resolutely swallowed the grief. Pushed it down with the betraying flicker of hope until they canceled each other out. "That's not going to happen and you know it. He's gone, and it's her fucking fault, whatever way you want to look at it."

"But what if it's not?" She wheedled upward past cajoling to desperation. "You've said yourself, everything about that time was crazy. Out of control. Like those noises? You remember how bad it got some nights, all the screaming and pounding and scratching? Banging from the third floor? And we saw things. You know we did, whether you want to remember or not."

He stared straight ahead, a blank wall where his memories should be. Which made sense, given the nature of growing up as a Lasco. "We saw what she wanted us to see."

6

Her voice grew brittle. "Speak for yourself. You weren't there every minute, you know. Maybe you can explain away some stuff, but you don't get to tell me I didn't experience what I did."

He paused for a beat, pursed his lips. "Okay. I'm sorry, I didn't mean to do that. I just don't want you buying into her delusion."

"But what if it really *was* something about that house? Everything got worse as soon as we moved in—*she* got worse. Isn't there any part of you that's curious about why?"

Nate counted to three, concentrating only on his breath. "No, because it wasn't the house, it was the circumstances. Her divorce, losing the child support from Dad, the breakup with Mark after that. Actually having to be responsible for herself and us. And she wasn't great before that." He paused, lowering his voice, striving for calm. "I won't try to diminish your fear, or what you might have seen when you were alone. But the other shit? That pounding? Those crazy noises? Don't you remember who was *never* around for that? None of this requires a paranormal investigator to explain. It was Stella. Only her."

"Please. You were as scared as the rest of us. What we experienced, there's no way it was just one person doing it. Even if it was Mom, there had to be something else at play. And anyway, that wasn't the only time. There was something there, something in that house that wasn't . . . right. Wasn't natural."

Nate worked on sounding kind, reeling in the temper that threatened to break loose at the slightest provocation. "You're right. It wasn't natural, the way Stella acted, how she treated us. And it's normal to want to find excuses, reasons why—"

She mowed over him like she hadn't heard a word. "You're telling me you don't remember *anything* weird from back then? No weird sounds or feelings? Anything that can't be explained by all that convenient logic of yours?"

7

He reflected for all of two seconds, coming up against that comfortably blank wall again. "No. I just remember a whole lot of fights and yelling and—" He stopped, closed his eyes as the sense memory came rolling over him, the dip in his gut that had become his constant companion during those dark days. *You're not a kid anymore, and she has no power over you.* His brain believed him, but his trauma reactions had a long ways to go.

"Shawn experienced it, too," she insisted. "You can write me off as being too young, but what about what he saw?"

Nate frowned, trying to conjure a recollection of what she was saying. "I remember him being . . . upset. In a lot of turmoil."

"Afraid," she said in a low voice.

"Sure. We all were. Of Stella. And with good reason, as it turned out."

"It wasn't just her. He was afraid of something else."

Nate gave a bitter laugh. "Yeah. He was afraid of himself, of who he might turn into. And that was Stella's fault, too."

"I don't understand. You think Shawn was afraid of *himself*?"

Of course she wouldn't remember. She'd been so little back then, too young for Shawn to take into his confidence. He'd rarely done so with Nate, once things got bad, but it had been enough. "It doesn't matter," he said finally. "It's not worth going into if you don't remember."

"Fine. So I don't remember that, and you don't remember what he saw, but *I* do, so don't discount his experiences, just because he's not here to voice them himself." She waited, only speaking again when it became clear he wouldn't. "You've really forgotten all of it, haven't you?"

"I haven't forgotten *shit*. I wish I had. But wishing doesn't do anyone any good, and neither does rewriting history to make yourself more comfortable." *That's what she does*. He almost said it, but held back with effort. Comparing his sister to their mother was a line he wouldn't cross, no matter how annoyed he was.

"I get it," she said softly. "That stuff was awful. I'm not saying she's totally blameless in everything that happened, but come on. It's simplistic to pretend there was nothing else."

When he didn't answer, she pushed on. "Please. I'm asking you do to this for me, if not for her. I need closure. Aury needs closure. So do you, whether you want to admit it or not. She says she won't do it unless all of us are there. Please don't cost us this."

Nate made an effort to loosen his tensed muscles, to let go of the poisonous spread of rage flooding his veins.

"I'm not the one who cost anyone *anything*. It wasn't my fault then, and it isn't now."

"I never said—"

"It doesn't matter. I know it's what everyone thinks, because it's always the whistle blower that's the problem, not the abusive malignant narcissist. But this is on her, and I'm done taking the fall for her shit. Even if Harper Lane was the most haunted house in the world, none of that's what killed Shawn. And if we never get closure—which, spoiler alert, we never fucking will—that's not on me."

He ended the call and stood gripping the phone, his knuckles white, palms sweaty. Knowing that no matter how many times he told himself his brother's death wasn't his fault, he'd never fully believe it.

# CHAPTER TWO

"**H**OW OLD WAS he when he passed?"

Nate cast his mentor a glance under dark brows, his shaggy hair slightly obscuring his view of her face. Not that it would have told him anything.

Carrie Barker exuded a pleasant, unruffled calm no matter what came her way. It was part of why he respected her, why he'd chosen to work with her once he'd completed his degree and clinicals. He'd looked up to her, awed at the time by her skill and intelligence, and it was a surprise when she accepted his application. She probably had plenty of applicants, and before she took Nate on, she'd operated a strictly solo practice. Several years into his work, he was no longer star struck, but he was still guilty of idealizing her. Her predictable, measured responses were a balm to his frayed nerves, conditioned to expect outbursts and erratic tempers. Sometimes, though, he just wanted someone to scream with. Someone who'd get as pissed as he was, shout at the heavens, punch things and get plastered. Carrie was never going to be that person, especially not with him. He told himself that was a good thing.

"Seventeen," he said, though she already knew the answer. They'd been over it so many times, but grounding him in details was part of her method, one he used with his own patients.

"That's very young."

"I know." He stared down at the carpet between his shoes, a bland but pleasant shade of blue.

"Do you remember him?"

"Of course I do. I was sixteen when he died, not six."

She waited until he leaned back against the unyielding chair and linked his hands on the back of his head. His hair was getting long back there, too—he'd need to get it cut, soon. The idea of making an appointment and finding the time to go exhausted him.

"Not as much as I'd like," he admitted. "Sometimes it gets hazy, and the memories . . . it's like they're fluid, or something. I remember some of the things we got up to together, holidays, but so much of it is the bad stuff."

*You've forgotten it all, haven't you?*

His stomach dipped as something gnawed at his hindbrain, an anxiety response without anything concrete to pin it to. Except . . . he wasn't imagining the dread. There was something there, lurking in his subconscious. A memory, or a dream. Something in the house . . . a shadow that shouldn't be there. Was Katy right? Had Shawn seen it? He could almost see his older brother telling him something important, something dire. But while he could picture Shawn's mouth moving, words leaving his lips, he couldn't hear his voice. It was almost certainly a manufactured memory, created in response to Katy's phone call, but it bothered him that he couldn't be sure. His palms grew sweaty and his breath quickened. He looked over his shoulder, almost expecting to see something looming, watching him.

Carrie's voice pulled him back from the edge.

"The stuff with Stella." Carrie respected his desire to distance himself, not affix the label of "mother" to someone he hated. "Stella didn't earn that title," she'd told him once, early in their working relationship, and it was incredible how freeing and validating those five words had been. It was a gift he sought to pay forward to the broken souls who came to him for help.

"Yeah. Stella. Always Stella."

She tilted her head. "It makes sense, though. Those

memories are tied to very strong emotions—fear and anger."

Nate leaned forward again and hunched his shoulders. "I know. But it pisses me off. Because I remember *that* shit, but not what his voice sounded like, which side he parted his hair on, or how his smile looked. I don't remember *him,* because there's no fucking air left once Stella enters the room."

"You remember that he loved you. That he protected you younger kids—that's important."

Nate's throat clogged with decades of unshed tears and he turned his head. "He shouldn't have had to. It's what got him killed."

"No. It's not."

His anger flared again, her calm certainty exacerbating his temper this time. "Yes, it fucking is. I don't care what the police report said, what lies they bought. It wasn't an accident, and he sure as shit didn't do it himself."

"I know," she said softly. She didn't, not for certain, but she'd long accepted Nate's assessment of what happened to his brother, and his anger cooled. "My point is, an older sibling looking out for the younger kids isn't a capital offense. Don't fall into her trap of making it anyone's fault but hers. He didn't make her do it, and neither did some entity."

"Yeah," he said, wondering why he felt so empty. Was there some small, pitiful part of himself that yearned for the kind of hope Katy carried? He thought he was long over mourning the parental love he'd never had.

Carrie seemed to read his mind, a knack of empathy. "Wasn't there anyone in your lives who stood up to Stella? I know your father wasn't around much, but what about an uncle or aunt, a teacher or a neighbor? Someone who saw what was going on?"

"Uncle Ron—Stella's brother—he'd swoop in from time to time, but it always felt like more of an obligation. I don't think he cared much for us."

"And he was the only one?"

Nate sighed. "For a while, Stella had this boyfriend. Mark. She dated a lot, but wasn't good at long term stuff. But Mark had better staying power than most."

Carrie smiled. "Good guy, then?"

He pursed his lips. "For a time, yeah. Everybody's got a threshold though, and Stella finally blew past his. He packed up and left and we never saw him again." He tried to sound breezy, like the bewildering loss of the only stable adult they'd ever known hadn't devastated the four of them. As though genuine care didn't leave a ragged hole in its absence, so much worse than before it warmed their lives.

Carrie let the silence ride for a minute. "I'm sorry, Nate. You didn't deserve that."

Nate cleared his throat. "Anyway. How'd the Peterson case go?"

"Quite well, thank you," she said, her expression closing off.

He chose not to take the hint. "Was it something external this time, like they thought? Or just more of the same?"

She studied him. "Is this professional interest, or personal?"

He scowled. "Neither. You know I don't believe in that stuff, and there's no way it applies to the infamous Lascos. We were fucked up enough without needing to blame it on ghosts and goblins."

"Mm hmm."

When she didn't continue, he sighed and looked up, attempting to effect nonchalance. "So what was the diagnosis? What crept through the halls of the Peterson house?" He added a little theater to the last sentence. If everything was a joke, then none of the answers mattered.

"It's gone. That's the only thing that matters. We're talking about you, Nate."

He pulled at a loose thread on his pants. She'd told him about the other side of her work, the paranormal stuff, and every so often she'd open up a bit about what she saw, but she'd never let him fully into her confidence. To his knowledge, she didn't let anyone in, but it didn't stop him from wanting to be the one. Even if he avoided acknowledging why that was.

"You feel guilty about Shawn's death," she said finally. "That's why you need to fixate on the protection aspect— that gives you license for endless flagellation."

His gaze snapped up to meet hers. "It wasn't my fault."

"*I* know that. So do your sisters, and likely whatever other friends or family you've told."

*Friends. Sure.*

"But you don't believe it yet."

He dropped his gaze back to the floor. "No. I guess not."

"What *do* you think they blame you for? You've mentioned being Stella's scapegoat. I thought it was Shawn who was always in trouble."

"He was. But not because he was some violent nutcase."

Carrie frowned. "Who claimed that? Stella?"

"Shawn, actually. He said he felt . . . tainted." He strove again to remember if his older brother ever mentioned any specific occurrences before he died, if he'd given a name to any fear beyond the label Stella saddled him with.

"Tainted, how?"

Nate rolled his neck to a chorus of crackling cartilage. "Stella had him convinced he was a shitty person. An irredeemable kid—dangerous. Violent."

Carrie's brows lifted. "That's pretty intense. What was her basis for that accusation?"

Nate laughed harshly. He could dissociate himself from his patients' experiences with no trouble, but the callous he'd developed over his own history was paper-thin. "That he had a temper. It was such a joke—he was a normal adolescent boy, with all the hormones that went with it. And anyway, parents in the eighties didn't feel it

14

incumbent on them to teach kids how to handle their emotions—we were always told to stop feeling anything that was inconvenient for them."

Carrie gave a fleeting smile. "Astute observation."

He refused to acknowledge the little thrill of pleasure that rolled through him at her mild praise. *Pathetic*. He roughened his voice and looked away. "It was all emotional manipulation. Even a perfectly adjusted adult would've had a hard time keeping calm with her. She'd push and prod and poke at him until he lost it, then there'd be that smug smile and she'd act like he'd just proven her case. Like him finally raising his voice to her when she's been screaming at him for an hour means he's dangerous." Nate huffed and dropped his gaze to his lap. "Eventually he bought into it—the bad shit's always easiest to believe."

"That's inexcusable on her part," Carrie said, a hint of rigidity in her jaw. It was nearly an emotional outburst on the Carrie scale, and it made Nate feel better, if only a little. She cocked her head. "Did he ever act on that anger, that you recall?"

He wanted to say no, to immediately refute the idea Shawn had any culpability. But as the confused morass of images and memory washed over him, there were slivers of his older brother's fury. Of his low-voiced threats uttered through clenched teeth. Hell, they'd all fantasized about giving Stella back her own, except possibly Katy, but that didn't mean any of them ever actually did anything. "No," he said after a minute, a stretch of time that felt like betrayal.

"Even if he had, it doesn't make him a bad person, or mean he bears any blame in what happened to him."

Nate looked up, frowning. "I know that."

"So Stella pushed his buttons, cast him in the role of violent teenage boy. But even with all that going on, he protected the three of you?"

"Yeah. He did. Even if we pissed him off, as soon as she came into the mix, it was all for one."

She smiled. "He sounds pretty wonderful, as brothers go."

Nate smiled back, but only briefly. "He was. Not perfect, by any means, but pretty great. As long as he was around, the rest of us were safe. It was always a game of who was on the outs, and after a while he just stayed there. Spared the rest of us, even if I didn't understand at the time." He took a breath. "But then he died, and she needed someone new to blame for everything that happened after."

"And that was you. Was that because you were next in line, age wise? Or because you were the only other male?"

He shrugged. "I'm the one who broke the silence. I told the cops everything, and the social workers after that. In a sense, I'm the one who broke up the family."

Carrie pursed her lips. "Which you know isn't the truth. Stella did that, with every choice she made."

"I know. I know I did the right thing, but—" He trailed off, wishing emotions responded to logic.

"Do you think it would help you, hearing what your mother has to say?"

Nate's temper flared and he pushed himself off the chair, took a few jerky turns around the office. "No. Everything that falls out of her mouth is a lie."

"I know. I guess I'm wondering what would happen if the three of you—you and your sisters—confronted her with what you know, what you remember. From what you tell me, she was very good at manipulating each of you individually. She kept you at each other's throats so you wouldn't recognize the strength you had in numbers. But you're adults now. You don't have to play the roles she assigned you, and she has no power over you. What do you think would happen if you go together, and refuse to let her control the narrative?"

"What would happen? *Nothing*. That's what. You know how it played out back then. She never even saw the inside of a jail after what she did—she's too good at playing her part. Give her ten minutes and she'll have a room full of strangers hanging on her every word. Nothing the three of us say is ever going to have any impact on her." He closed his eyes against a memory, from when he didn't know, of begging her tearfully for something, and she wouldn't even look up, acknowledge he was there. He felt again that child's despair of helplessness, taken aback by the force of it.

Carrie's voice scattered the hurt, brought him back to the present. "Why do you think she's doing this? Why now? What's changed?"

Nate sighed and went to the single window, rested a hand on the pane. "If I had to guess? She wants something. And there's only two things that motivate that woman: money, and the damn limelight."

# CHAPTER THREE

"**IT'S BOTH, ACTUALLY.**" Nate's eldest sister Aurelia perched on the bar stool next to his, swinging one leg, the other hooked onto the lowest rung. "She's getting paid to do it. And you know she can't wait to be the center of attention again. How else is she supposed to score her dopamine?" She leaned in to take a sip of her coke. It wasn't a mixer, only soda and ice in her glass, but the way she treated it you'd think it was the most divine sin ever committed.

Nate eyed his own empty glass, wishing his vices were half as innocuous, but stuck to shelling peanuts and crushing the fragile bits beneath his thumb. It felt good to smash something. "You seem pretty calm about it."

She raised an eyebrow but didn't answer. It was a stupid thing to say—Aury floated a good three feet above the rest of the world, looking down on it with impassive grace. She was never anything but calm, but she lacked Carrie's warmth.

"Katy's a sweetheart, but she's nuts to let Stella do this to her again. We're not getting any answers." When Aury didn't respond, he leaned toward her, eyes narrowing. "You do get that, right? No matter who comes or doesn't, she's not going to tell us the truth."

Aury lifted one elegant shoulder and stole two peanuts from the ever-growing stack at his elbow. "Maybe. Maybe not. And maybe we can help her along."

Nate cocked his head. "Help her along? What does that mean?"

His sister smiled down at the bartop. "There are more things on heaven and earth . . . "

"Oh come on, don't pull that enigmatic middle child shit."

She laughed. "I'm just saying. This is an opportunity for all of us."

He frowned. "An opportunity for what? You're not seriously buying into any of this supernatural bullshit, are you?"

She ignored him. "You know why she's so keen on it."

Nate frowned. "Stella?"

She shook her head, her dark bob falling over one eye. "Katy. She needs this. Or at least, she thinks she does."

He eyed her. "Why?"

Aury blew the hair out of her eyes and signaled the bartender for another soda. "She's getting married."

Nate sat back, mouth open, fingers frozen around a half-broken peanut shell. "*What*? Since when? And to who?"

She smiled. "You really don't get out much, do you? She got engaged a month or so ago, to a very nice man she's been dating named Tim."

It was his turn to raise a brow. "Very nice?"

"Shocking, right? Anyway, he's got two kids, pretty young ones. He's a widower."

The air went out of Nate's lungs. "Oh."

"Yeah. Oh."

"I guess that explains why she didn't tell me," he said, with another longing glance at the ice melting in his otherwise empty highball.

"Sure," said Aury, and left it at that, not bothering to sound like she believed him.

They sat in silence for a minute or so, Aury thinking Aury thoughts while Nate came to grips with what his youngest sister was doing. They'd spoken of it often enough, in the years since they'd moved out and found their own freedom. Sometimes he thought it was the only common ground they had, bitching about Stella and how bad she'd fucked them up. How none of them ever wanted kids, because they couldn't guarantee what would happen, what kind of parents they'd be. They'd only ever been shown the wrong way, their emotional development severely stunted. Nate's temper worried him—he'd never knowingly hurt anyone, especially a child, but what if it was something he couldn't control? What if there was some genetic beast coiled around his heart, ready to wake and cause chaos as soon as he let his guard down? He treated plenty of patients with anger issues, ones who'd continued cycles of abuse with their own kids. He refused to give himself a chance to cause that kind of damage.

His sisters felt the same, or at least they said they did. For Aury it was no hardship—she didn't like dating, or spending time with people. Nate had sometimes wondered if she were asexual, if she might find comfort or identity in the label. But he couldn't picture himself asking, and in any case the idea of being tied to another human was anathema to her, sex or not. But for Katy, it had been a sacrifice. She'd shed tears over it, but never once wavered. None of them wanted to become Stella, and the best way to prevent it was to take a different path at every turn. Now it seemed Katy was going back on their promise.

Aury pursed her lips. "I know what we said. And it's still true for me, but it seems shitty for Katy to have to keep paying the price when she didn't do anything wrong."

Nate watched her, trying to suss what she really thought about Katy's defection. "And she thinks it'll be . . . safe?"

Aury shrugged. "She needs it to be. She wants this. Wants a chance to do better, to believe she won't always be in Stella's shadow. And people do it all the time—break the cycle."

Nate sighed, bits of peanut shell scattering across the scarred bar top. "So, what? She thinks if she can prove it wasn't really our mother who killed Shawn, made our lives hell, that it was some fucking ghost or demon or haunted house or whatever, then she can skip into parenthood with no concerns?"

Aury smiled. "Well, yeah."

Nate raised an eyebrow. "And you're going along with this?"

Her smile dropped and she faced forward. "I am. But not for her—at least not entirely. I've got my own dragons to slay."

The hint of steel in her voice was the closest he'd heard to emotion in their adult lives. He didn't pursue the opening that wasn't really an opening—they might not be as close as some siblings, but he knew her well enough not to push. He didn't bother asking if Aury was funding the wedding, either. She always slipped money to their sister, her job as a forensic accountant leaving her with plenty of disposable income.

He waited a minute or two before speaking again, aiming for a certain dry humor. "At least you're not trying to tell me it really was ghosts that fucked up our lives back then."

Aury bit her bottom lip, didn't meet his eye. "No, it was Stella. I know that. But I'm not convinced it was only her."

Nate felt the ground slip beneath his feet. "What, not you, too? You're drinking the Kool-Aid on this shit? The house wasn't haunted. It was just a house, and Stella can't hide behind it."

She set her jaw. "You weren't there as long as I was. Things happened there. Things I don't fully remember, but . . ."

He sighed. "Yeah, that's trauma for you."

She straightened, slid the mask back in place, and Nate felt regret too late. Aury made herself vulnerable to him, and instead of listening, he dismissed her fears. Who did that sound like?

"Anyway," she continued, back to dull and bored. "I want to see the old place. It's been a long time, and I want to know if it feels the same as it did. If there's any of that atmosphere left, or if we brought it with us."

The bottom dropped out of his stomach. "The house? She's going back to the house?"

Aury pursed her lips. "We all are, dearest brother. It's where they're filming. Didn't you know?"

# CHAPTER FOUR

**N**ATE'S **HANDS** **TREMBLED** over his keyboard as he logged into his old email, one he never checked but kept active for family he wanted nothing to do with and spam email subscriptions. He botched the password twice, searching his memory for what combination he'd used back then. It was funny—what he chose for each new account always seemed like the biggest part of his world at the time, something he'd never forget. But he could only assume his attention was more transient than most. The things that were important to him were a steady parade in and out of his life, which resulted in a shit ton of irritating password resets.

Once he got in it was an easy matter to track down the message. It was from the production company, who charmingly called themselves "The Cleaners." Nate wondered if it was a reference to *Poltergeist*, and if so, did that mean they fancied themselves more than journalists? What the hell was the plan beyond exploitation stories about fucked-up people who'd done fucked-up things and wanted someone else to blame?

He skimmed past the introductory paragraphs, skipping to the link Aury had told him he'd find.

"It's wild," she'd said, paying the tab and slinging her purse over her shoulder. "And kind of infuriating, so maybe don't watch it before you have to be around people."

He'd taken her advice to heart, waited until he was home with a covert glass of scotch on the rocks. It was above and beyond the one a day he allowed himself, but these were extenuating circumstances.

The trailer opened with a closeup of his mother's face, half in shadow, her head dipped low. "My name is Stella Lasco, and twenty years ago, a ghost cost me my entire family."

Nate sucked in a breath, powerless against the stupefied fury that swept through him. "Yeah, sure, it was a ghost. Anything to shift responsibility." He tossed back a third of his drink and choked against the burn until he couldn't tell if it was the alcohol or incandescent rage that set his chest on fire.

The shot zoomed out and she lifted her chin, bringing her out of shadow. There was no longer any protection from her wide, bloodshot gaze, the vapid expression, lips just parted in an almost-convincing imitation of actual emotional pain. "But I'm not taking it lying down anymore. I want my kids back, and I'll go through hell to get them."

An excessively loud thunder sound effect boomed through the laptop speakers in tandem with a lightning logo reading: *The Cleaners!*

Nate jumped in his seat then glared at the screen. If nothing else did it, that stupid exclamation point in the title convinced him these people were hacks. The voiceover that followed cemented his impression.

"I'm Helter Scanlon, founder of *The Cleaners!*"

Oh, God. He even pronounced the exclamation. Nate closed his eyes, but snapped them open again when the young man continued.

"This week we're going to battle for Stella Lasco, a lonely mother of three whose life was ruined by the house you see behind me."

*Mother of three?* Bile rose in Nate's throat, or maybe it was the scotch threatening to come back up. Three. She couldn't even acknowledge Shawn had once existed? Nate was livid, each vicious stab like an injection of pure anger right to his heart.

"A mansion of misery if I ever saw one—hey, Gunther?"

The camera moved up and down with a nod and Nate considered smashing his laptop.

"We don't know what awaits us beyond those doors—2103 Harper Lane hasn't been occupied for at least a decade, and those who have dared to go inside are marked by its darkness."

The kid's attempt at gravity fell flat, but Nate barely noticed. The camera panned wide again, zoomed in behind "Helter" to show a familiar brick facade that made his breath catch. The arched wooden front door was faded, sagging in its frame, one of the small windows at the top smashed through. The front yard was overgrown and weed-choked, the steps crumbling.

Nate waited, not breathing. Were they going inside? Would they open that door, the one that led down dark halls and up staircases on a path that ended at the *other* door? His throat grew tight, his lungs aching to draw breath but he couldn't make himself. He needed to see, to know.

"Take a journey with us into the very worst kind of haunting." The camera cut away to Helter again. "The kind that can cost you your very soul."

Another canned thunder effect and the trailer ended.

Nate sat there feeling stunned, trying to reel himself in, but instead of fury bursting forth he found himself laughing. It wasn't a happy sound, manic and too loud.

"Her *soul*? She thinks that *house* cost her a *soul*? You can't lose what you never had." His laughter wouldn't stop, bubbled up and over until his stomach hurt and tears rolled down his cheeks. When he could breathe again, he downed the rest of his drink and rose on shaky legs to pour himself another.

"Oh, you bitch," he whispered to the blank screen. "I won't let you stand up there and whitewash him out of existence." Carrie was right—he couldn't let Stella control the narrative. He'd tried to move past it, to forgive her for his own sake, for his sanity. It had always been lip service. Every time he tried, he couldn't get past the last time he saw his brother, the blood trickling over his eye, the look of determination on his face. Filled with the mistaken belief he could ever get the upper hand with a narcissist.

It was time the world knew what kind of mother Stella was. And *past* time she paid for her crimes. Aury was right—they all had dragons to slay, and he wasn't going to miss his opportunity.

An unpleasant smile curled his lips as he composed his response to "Helter" the cleaner, accepting the invitation.

"Be there with bells on," he whispered as he hit send and closed the laptop. Then he proceeded to drink himself into oblivion, letting his memories slide into the deep dark of a blackout drunk. The last thing he saw before he passed out was the empty bottle on his nightstand, and a blunted version of shame prodded him ineffectually.

"I was doing so good," he slurred, and lost consciousness. Regret was a problem for tomorrow.

# CHAPTER FIVE

**A SOUND HE** couldn't place or understand pulled Nate from troubled sleep. It was a deep and heavy noise, somehow grinding, and he couldn't picture what might make it. He tried to sit up, to reach for the light, but found he couldn't move. His eyes were open, searching the darkness, trying to adjust, but he couldn't influence any other part of his body, including his breathing.

Fuck. That was always the worst part of sleep paralysis—the slow, even breaths of unconsciousness weren't enough for his waking mind. The loop of sound that had woken him continued: a low-toned scraping that thrummed in his bones, felt like a weight on his chest. It enhanced the feeling of suffocation, and he fought to keep from panicking—he'd been through this, many times. He just had to get the smallest part moving, and the spell would break.

He worked on his left pinky, putting all his minimal strength into making it wiggle. It wouldn't budge, and worse than that, it felt as though something bound it, pressed against the digit with a weight that held it fast.

The sounds grew louder, rising from all corners of the room, and his lungs burned with the effort of getting enough oxygen. He kept telling himself it was a dream, the hallucination of a mind caught halfway between sleep and consciousness, but that didn't make it any less scary. He redoubled his efforts to move his finger, pressing back against what bound him as hard as he could.

A weight settled at the end of the bed, dipping the mattress, something solid next to his feet. His breath came faster, but just as shallow as he fought harder to move. It felt real, so fucking real, but if he could just move it would go away.

Still trapped, he struggled as whatever it was slid up the mattress, pressing itself close. Its weight crushed him as it moved from his legs to his hips and up to his stomach. It was heavy, compressing his flesh and organs, and he panicked at the thought of what would happen if it reached his lungs. He'd suffocate—positional asphyxia, his body slowly draining of oxygen as the weight of an alien presence pressed him ever further down into the unforgiving mattress. You couldn't die in a dream, and even in his erratic state he knew that, but locked as he was, at the thing's mercy, he could no longer control his fear.

He screamed in the distorted voice of a dreamer, the sharpness of his cries for help muffled through his closed mouth, but still he could not wake up. His eyes the only thing he could move, he rolled his gaze around the dark bedroom, looking for salvation. There was none. He lived alone, the condo he shared a wall with was on the other side of the house, and anyway he didn't know the older couple who'd moved in a year ago. He didn't know any of his neighbors, and usually he liked it that way. But tonight, there was no one to hear his screams.

A shadow, darker than the rest, hovered over him as whatever creature shared his bed made it up to his face. He felt hot, ragged breath against his cheek, loose hairs stirring and tickling his forehead. He struggled to escape, to make himself sit up, but his body wouldn't obey. He didn't recall an episode of sleep paralysis ever lasting so long, or being this tactile. He could feel *everything*.

Eyes dry and aching, he managed to focus his vision enough to stare just in front of his face, to seek what pinned him there with such cruelty. Whatever it was, it didn't move. Not the slightest shift or raise of its chest with breath. He could see the curve of a shoulder, an outline of shaggy hair at the nape.

Something touched his lips, rough and rank, pinching his mouth so it pooched out like a duck bill. Nate's gaze swung wild but all he saw were two burning halos of blue flame. They hissed to life inches from his face, illuminating a dark-lipped mouth opened wide in a ghastly grin. For the space of a heartbeat he felt a tickle of memory, a nagging belief he'd been here before, seen just this thing. Those lips, those eyes, the inky shadow of something watching close and waiting for him to move. Then the features resolved themselves into something else entirely, and Nate found himself staring at a viciously smiling version of himself.

*"Time for a homecoming, Natey boy,"* ground a voice in his ear. Agony ripped through his face as another reeking hand joined the first, jamming into his mouth, pulling the sides in opposite directions til he felt the skin of his face splitting, separating bit by bit. Each second he was convinced would be the last, that surely he would fully wake, heart thudding, the pain and certainty of the dream fading, but it went on and on. He felt the pull and tear of rending flesh reach up to the corners of his eyes and all he could do was scream, until the dream took even that away.

The nightmare version of himself leaned closer, shoving its hands into his too-wide mouth up to the elbow, choking off his cries. The arms filled his throat, cutting off what little air he'd been able to get, slipping further and further. He felt his esophagus widen, his jaws crack and dislocate, a searing pain as the arms just kept coming. Vision going black from lack of oxygen, he could somehow see the tail end of the Nate thing wriggling in, disappearing down his throat. Settling in and filling his belly with alien movement.

It was inside him, now, while he suffocated, hot tears trickling from the corners of his eyes, stinging the open wound of his split face. He waited to die, to be freed from the agony, to escape his earthly prison. He gave a gurgling scream and found the spell had broken, he could move again, but the pain didn't end. It stayed with him as he rolled ponderously to his side, his gut distended, the flesh of his stomach stretched and tearing. He groaned and made it to the bathroom on his knees, the torn flaps of his cheeks swaying with each movement.

When he felt cool tile beneath his palms, he reached for the commode to pull himself up, stretching for the light switch. The movement pulled the skin of his sides past their breaking point and he felt an insidious tear run from his hips to his ribcage. He screamed but managed to flip the light on. Yet the burn of illumination didn't stop it, only revealing the extent of his maiming. He moaned and looked away from his stomach, transferring his hands to the vanity and pushing up with all his might. His only thought was to catch sight of himself in the mirror, though a sickening dread filled him at what he might see. And when he did manage it, when he'd dragged his heavy, unwieldy body high enough to meet his own eyes, he screamed. For above the shredded remains of his face burned two bright blue lights, and whatever now looked out at the world from Nate's eyes did so with its own dark plans in mind.

# CHAPTER SIX

**N**ATE STOOD AT the end of the freshly asphalted driveway that led to his two-story condo. New construction, no prior residents, he'd bought it five years before, at a good time in the housing market. He huddled into his navy pea coat, the collar turned up against the chill, but never so much as considered going back inside to wait. He didn't know who'd be coming in the hired car, and had no desire to let anyone over his threshold, family or no. He needed his spaces clear, unblemished by negative energy or shitty memories. Nothing bad was allowed to happen in his home.

Except those dreams, which he could do nothing about. The first had been the worst—he hadn't woken til morning, his face and jaw aching, feeling like he'd spent the night in struggle instead of rest. It had been so vivid, he'd expected to wake up on the bathroom floor in a pool of blood, if he woke up at all. He didn't remember making it back to bed from the bathroom, which made sense, as that had been part of the dream, too. His throat ached terribly, his voice a rasping whisper. Likely that had been what spawned the dream—he was coming down with something, and his subconscious had made use of it. It should have been a comforting conclusion, but it wasn't.

He'd never slipped back into unconsciousness after an episode of sleep paralysis before—he'd always gotten his head above water, grounded himself in reality before trying to sleep again. He'd certainly never dreamed a wake up before, a false reprieve where he could move again but the nightmare continued around him. When he could make himself enter the bathroom that morning, he was terrified to raise his eyes to the mirror, but his body was the same size it had been when he'd gone to bed, and his face was still intact, just sore. He traced his finger along a thin fold in his flesh that mimicked the pattern of his dream torture, but it was just a temporary wrinkle from the bed sheet where his face had pressed. He shuddered, remembering the stir of something in his belly, and put his hands on his gut protectively. Same as always, the only movement he felt was the roil of stomach acid and gas. All day long, though, he avoided his reflection, afraid of what he'd see in his own eyes. A dream, obviously, despite the slight and nagging tug of recognition, one vivid enough to stick with him, so he indulged himself, figuring it would fade with time.

But nothing faded, not for Nate. Propped up each night by another episode, every dream featured him committing horrible atrocities, hurting and maiming the people he loved. He always felt out of control in the dreams, like he was watching the world from a small window in his mind. He beat his fists against it, screamed in silence for it to stop, for whatever was driving his body to give him back control. And each one ended the same, staring into his own reflection, seeing only blue flames where his eyes should be. As with the first, he couldn't escape it, couldn't wake himself up or sink back into dreamless slumber.

The worst part of the dreams was the pleasure that seeped through him when he stopped fighting, threatening to consume the horror he felt with satisfaction. The relief he felt in giving in to whatever controlled his dream self, followed swiftly by exhilaration. He told himself he wasn't guilty of what happened in his subconscious, but he never could resist one more reason to hate himself.

A sleek black SUV pulled up to the curb, sounding an unnecessary honk that sent an ice pick of pain through his head, in the sensitive spot on his eyebrow, just above his nose. He winced, the ache resonating through his body, the uneasy peace he'd made with his hangover threatened by a wave of nausea. He'd been drinking to blackout every night for the past week, each morning promising himself he'd do better. But since talking to his sisters, and watching that God-awful trailer, all he could see was Stella. Her woeful expression, her simpering mouth. It kept his nerves raw, his emotions on edge. The only time he was able to forget her, forget the ordeal that awaited him, was when he was drunk, or with a patient. And the profession frowned on taking patients home, even as a talisman against painful memories, so scotch it was. Besides, he needed it to sleep, the dread of those dreams keeping him awake unless he was blitzed.

Last night had been the worst binge so far, but he'd been so keyed up, rehearsing what he wanted to say, having imaginary arguments like some kind of choose-your-own-adventure from hell. Stella always managed to catch him off guard, leave him reeling and off balance, the right responses never coming until it was far too late. He wouldn't let her do it this time. He had things to say, to bring to light, and he'd be damned if he let her do it to him or his sisters again.

Nate squinted at the SUV's tinted windows, looking for confirmation that this was his ride. The tint was so dark he couldn't see a thing beyond the glass, and finally the passenger window rolled down, revealing a huge blond man with spiked hair and sunglasses leaning into his sight line.

"Hey man, you getting in or what?"

Nate stared at the guy, unable to place him. He'd been expecting Helter, from the trailer. "Uh, you with the show?"

The man nodded and smiled, reached a hand out. "Sorry, forgot. Not used to driving something fancy with all this tint. I'm Gunther."

Nate leaned through the window to shake his hand, studying the vibrant sleeve of blue and green tattoos with envy. He'd always wanted one, but never managed to pull the trigger. He wanted it to mean something, but his loves, human and inanimate alike, were ephemeral, escaping any kind of consistency.

His sluggish mind caught up to the social niceties and he cleared his throat. "Uh, Nathan Lasco."

Gunther nodded and gestured to the back door. "I know. Got your sisters in here already." He studied Nate's face for a beat or two, then held a hand up. "Hang on a sec." He popped the glove box and rummaged around before offering Nate a bottle of ibuprofen.

Nate took the bottle with real gratitude, dumping out a handful and swallowing them down with the rest of his tepid coffee.

Katy launched herself across the middle row when he opened the door, nearly knocking him off his feet. He swallowed back bile and returned her fierce hug.

"Hey, kiddo, good to see you." He winced, wondering what had possessed him to say it. Shawn had always been the one to call Katy "kiddo."

If she noticed, she didn't say anything, but pulled him into the vehicle and resumed what sounded like an endless flow of chatter, addressed to the occupants at large, or no one at all. Satisfied that Gunther was nodding along, Nate settled in the back with Aury, whose greeting was much more subdued.

"You okay?" she asked. "You look shittier than usual."

"Fine. Bad dreams, that's all."

She didn't respond and he leaned back against the seat. Eyes closed, he shoved his hands deep in his pockets, closing them around the airplane bottle of scotch hidden in each. He was damned sure he'd need a shot or two before this day was over, especially if he followed through with what he had planned.

*I will. I'm not chickening out this time.*

34

Katy and Gunther's bright patter began to wear on him, his youngest sister's sunny demeanor pulling yet another new friend into her orbit, though he was glad not to hear any wheeze in her breathing. He tuned out the sounds of the car and willed the painkillers to kick in.

By the time his headache eased, anxiety rose to take its place. His stomach roiled with nerves, his palms sweating more with each passing mile. It was a forty-five-minute drive out to the old place, and by the thirty mark he could hardly breathe. It was always this way—he avoided this road whenever possible, unable to convince his body he had no intention of revisiting his own personal hell. This time he didn't even try—maybe his subconscious had known all along.

Aury took his hand and squeezed it. "I know."

He straightened in his seat and flashed her a brief smile, thankful she was there. It was a thing he forgot in his isolation, that there were two people on this planet who shared the same genes and fucked-up memories with him. It was a balm, being in their presence, knowing whatever he remembered they could, and more importantly *would,* corroborate.

"Are *you* okay?" he asked belatedly. The give and take of concern wasn't something that came easy to him, outside of a professional setting.

"I'm fine," she said, letting go of his hand. She rubbed her arms, pulling in on herself.

Nate frowned. "Are you sure? You said before, about being scared here . . . " He cleared his throat. "Does it worry you?"

She shrugged. "Not as much as it used to. I know a lot more than I did back then."

His brows came together, which was enough to spike his headache. "Like what?" he asked through clenched teeth, swallowing back the surge of nausea.

She cast a glance at the seat ahead of them, then leaned in close. "Don't worry so much, okay? I've got some . . . plans in place. This isn't going to go how she expects."

Nate frowned. "Plans? What kind of plans?"

She tilted her head in the direction of their sister and gave a brief shake. *Not in front of the littlest.* Then she sat back and made a visible effort to relax. "Is this your first time back?" she asked in a louder voice.

Nate wiped his hands on his jeans, resisting the urge to press her for details. He'd spent most of his life trying not to think about Stella, but now there was an urgency to it, and the thoughts consumed his waking hours. "Yeah. I could never . . . make myself. And I didn't see the point."

Aury nodded, looked out the window, her body swaying with the car's movements. He didn't ask her the same question—he knew she'd been back, plenty, even if he'd never understood why.

"Did you . . . " He stopped, throat dry.

She turned back to him. "Did I what?"

He studied her impassive face, dark sunglasses hiding her eyes and her thoughts. She'd worked remotely for years, but she'd never been one for dressing up, anyway. She wore no makeup, and her short dark hair was pulled into a pony-nub, as she called it. A smattering of acne at her hairline was the only thing out of place.

"Have you been in since? In *there*, I mean? Did you ever, you know, while you were living there?"

Aury turned away again. After The Day of the Door, after Nate opened the flood gates and their lives were swarmed with a procession of cops and social workers, a judge had removed Katy from Stella's care, but given the older two a choice. So while Nate and Katy returned to the care of their cold and distant father, Aury chose to stay. Dad was an asshole, but his disinterest and neglect was infinitely preferable to Stella's unpredictable fury. They'd all given up on a normal childhood by then, and getting away became their singular goal.

Nate again felt that kick of guilt—in a way, he was the reason they'd been split up. The Lasco kids had been raised to keep every family secret, never let outsiders in, and the instinct was buried deep. He didn't know what his sisters told all those blank-faced authority figures back then: they'd never discussed it among themselves. It bothered him that Aury went back to their mother, like it lent the woman legitimacy she didn't deserve.

"No," she answered finally. "It was taped shut when we got back, I guess the cops left it that way. We never bothered to cut it off."

He closed his eyes against the tide of images that crowded to the forefront. The defiant fury on Shawn's face as he led the way to his own death, tears of anger running down his cheeks mingling with blood from his brow, his teeth bared in a snarl. The smug look of satisfaction Stella cast the three who were left behind as she slammed and locked the door. The burn of her open-handed slaps still hot on his cheek, wrist throbbing where she'd yanked him into line. The screams of his sisters, and the insidious certainty they would never see their brother alive again. They'd lived like that for so long, with no expectation of safety, and in spite of all the work he'd done on himself, those days still manifested when he winced from sudden yelling, or his heart raced when a door slammed. When he'd gotten older and learned that not everyone grew up dreading what line their parents would cross and leave them dead, he'd been incredulous.

"You're gonna bleed all over the leather," murmured Aury, and Nate opened his eyes, followed her gaze to his clenched fists. He uncurled his fingers with effort and wiped crescent moons of welling blood on his jeans.

"This could be good for us, Nate. All of us. If I didn't believe that, I wouldn't be here. But if this is too much, I can handle it. Handle her."

Nate snorted. "Don't make the same mistake we used to. Don't believe she's a problem that *can* be handled."

She didn't acknowledge his words, still pressing her point. "I'm serious. You don't have to do this."

Nate sniffed and rolled his shoulders, taking deep

breaths. He hadn't even been trying to keep himself calm and grounded, forgetting all his training in the face of his dread. He gave her a small smile. "Obviously I do."

By the time the SUV pulled into the circular drive, Nate was sure he would puke. Even Katy went quiet, her profile towards him as she stared up at the house where their childhoods ended. She'd only been ten, Nate remembered, and his heart hurt, thinking of the little girl she'd been. He would do what he had to do for her. She'd been the one to lose the most that day—well, the most after Shawn.

Gunther opened the doors for the siblings without speaking, seeming to understand the gravity of the situation. They filed out one by one and stood looking up at the crumbling brick facade, the broken glass, the remaining windows dark and coated with grime, revealing nothing about what lay beyond. The house looked its worst at this season, all the wild growth of the past decades shriveled and dormant, hugging the bricks in straggling vines. It certainly looked like the stereotypical haunted house, but the dull fear that crowded his belly had nothing to do with ghosts.

Nate turned to Gunther, unloading equipment in silence. "That video—the episode trailer. You said no one had lived here for the past ten years."

Gunther nodded. "That was Helter, but yeah, I'm the one who does the research. It's been empty for a little over that."

Nate frowned. "I thought people were in and out of it—that's what your buddy said. That they'd all had strange experiences, and no one would stay." He wished he'd let Aury talk that night at the bar. "I'd never heard any of that—did you interview any of the prior tenants?"

The other man's jaw tightened and he glanced around, then offered a sheepish smile. "Uh, I'm not actually sure how much of that is true. That might have been Helter's idea of artistic license."

Nate's gaze narrowed. "Does Stella know that?"

"I'm sure he'll tell her after we're done."

Nate ground his teeth, seething. These clueless kids had just added fuel to the fire—Stella could teach a master class in gaslighting, mostly because it didn't take much for her to create and believe in a whole new reality. Especially if it was more palatable than the truth.

They couldn't know that, though. He reminded himself that most people weren't forced to think ten steps ahead in childhood just to survive. He made an effort to sound calm. "Then who owns it now?"

Gunther shrugged, not meeting his eyes. "That's complicated. I'm not good with like, title searches, man. There's trusts and deeds and whatever, so it's not real clear."

"But whoever it is, they're okay with you doing this? With us being here?"

The other man nodded, shouldering a boom mic. "Seem to be."

It wasn't an answer, and Nate was about to ask him to elaborate when Katy shouted his name from across the yard.

He turned, heart pounding, expecting to see both his sisters at his side, but only Aury stood there, lost in her own thoughts, staring up at the half-story at the top of the house. He wouldn't follow her gaze—not yet. He wasn't ready for the third floor.

Katy crouched much further away, her blonde head bent. She was too close to the house, right up on the foundation, and fear washed through him. He didn't believe for a second the place was haunted, but couldn't quash the irrational feeling the earth would yawn open, rolling his little sister into the house's gaping maw, stealing another of the Lasco kids before he could do anything.

"Nate, come look at this," she called again.

He jogged to her side, the fastest he could manage in his condition, and he suddenly regretted going into this impaired. He should be lighter on his feet, clearheaded if he was going to anticipate Stella's machinations.

"Don't run off like that," he admonished his sister when he reached her side, grimacing against the dull ache in his head that returned with the effort of running.

She raised an eyebrow, one side of her mouth turned up. He blushed, realizing how he sounded.

"Sorry," he muttered.

"It's fine," she said, the smile reaching the rest of her mouth. "Hard not to fall into old roles now we're here, isn't it?"

"I fucking hope not. What'd you want to show me?"

She parted a clump of tall, brown grass and pointed at something that stuck up from the earth, dirty and bent. "Do you recognize this?"

Nate crouched beside her, knees immediately voicing a complaint. When he realized what he was looking at, he fell back on his ass.

Aury came crunching over through the long-dead leaves and peered over their shoulders. "It's a knife," she observed.

"We know that, Aury," said Katy, a hint of annoyance in her voice. "Is it . . . was it one of his?"

Nate leaned closer, but he didn't need to. He just wanted to see it again, make sure it didn't disappear.

"Yeah," he croaked from a dry throat. "That's Shawn's, but I'll be damned if I know how it got here."

Gunther approached, stopping a respectful distance away. "Coulda just dropped it, right?" he suggested. "Maybe nobody saw it til now."

"That seems unlikely," said Aury in a flat voice.

"It's—it's the one—from that day," choked Nate. "The one they thought he used . . . that she *claimed* he used . . . for her . . . "

Gunther covered his mouth. "The fingers?"

"Yeah." Nate's gorge rose; he tore his gaze away from the knife.

# THE DAY OF THE DOOR

Aury's eyes were shadowed behind the sunglasses she still wore. "The one he was buried with."

Nate turned his head and vomited.

# CHAPTER SEVEN

**"H**OW'D YOU KNOW?" Nate asked Aury in a low voice.

They sat together on the bumper of the SUV, soaking in what sunshine they could. Aury glanced over her shoulder to where Katy sat with Gunther on the front step, pouring out some tearful story while the big man nodded, his brows knit, a hand on her shoulder. Nate bit his tongue against the knee-jerk urge to stop her, remind her not to air their dirty laundry. That was one of Stella's tricks, a manipulation to make them keep their mouths shut about what happened at home, and even after his own divergence, silence was still his instinct. Besides, soon enough Gunther would know all there was to know about their family.

"Another Katy conquest," Aury said, a smile in her voice.

"Answer me, Aury."

She shrugged. "I saw you do it. Open the casket and put the knife in with him."

He frowned. "Why'd you never say anything?"

"Why didn't you?"

He dropped his gaze to his bent knees, bouncing with the jiggle of his feet on the gravel. He gripped them hard, forcing himself to stop moving. "I figured I'd get in trouble. Maybe even go to jail."

She frowned. "For putting a keepsake in your brother's coffin?"

"I wasn't supposed to have it. They hadn't cleared it yet, from evidence. I . . . I stole it."

She considered this. "Doesn't say much for the integrity of the investigation, that a sixteen-year-old boy could just walk in and take evidence from an open homicide case."

Nate pursed his lips and spat, the sour taste of bile lingering at the back of his throat. "They didn't even consider homicide as a possibility. I can guarantee the two options were accident or suicide, no matter how much they had to twist themselves in knots to explain away the inconsistencies. I knew how it would be, so one of the times they left me alone, maybe the third or fourth day of questioning, I snuck off." He looked at the ground. "I couldn't stand the thought of his stuff rotting away in some box no one would ever look at. He had it that day . . . he only took it to feel safe. And when I thought about him, alone in the ground . . . I wanted him to have it." He forced a laugh to cover the deep well of pain. "Anyway, I don't think anyone gave too much of a shit, given who the victim was. A seventeen-year-old delinquent with anger problems? We saw how that played out."

"Hm."

"I'm not sorry. They'd already tested it as much as they were going to."

"No one said you should be."

"I mean, I don't think it affected anything. I don't give a fuck about the blood they found on it. He didn't use it on her. He didn't do that to her hand."

"It wasn't just blood," she said, voice flat.

Nate frowned. "What do you mean?"

"They found tissue, as well. Quite a bit."

He closed his eyes against the picture that rose in his mind, of a blade coated in his brother's blood, gobs of his flesh gathered at the hilt. His gorge rose but he managed to choke it down this time. "That doesn't mean shit."

"Mm." Her tone remained non-committal and his irritation flared.

"You don't believe that bullshit, do you? That Shawn would seriously hold her down and saw her fingers off? He was the one screaming, remember? Up until he couldn't." He shuddered, pushing out the echo of his brother's pain, the horrible sounds of impacts on flesh. All the injuries he'd pictured over the years, the imagined horror of how Shawn looked at the end. "He couldn't have, not without dulling the blade all to hell. She'd have had to sit still for it, let him do it. Somehow I don't see that happening."

"Stella certainly believes it," she said.

"That doesn't make it true," he replied harshly, ready to fight.

She finally met his eyes. "Of course not. It rather argues the opposite."

Nate sat back. "Right, sorry. I forget . . . "

"That not everything's a pitched battle? Yeah, hard habit to break."

"How the fuck did it get here, anyway?" he asked, looking back at the spot in the yard where they'd left the knife, an upside-down coffee cup acting as a half-assed evidence marker. Nate didn't know why they'd bothered, it wasn't as though anyone was going to come take statements and investigate the case of the reappearing knife. Gunther was keen on leaving it where it was until Helter arrived, at least.

"Million-dollar question and all that," Aury said, her eyes on the sky. Unlike him, she didn't glance down the road every ten seconds. Maybe she didn't mind waiting for Stella—she'd had the most practice at it, after all.

Nate pushed off the bumper, walked to the end of the drive and peered in either direction. "Where the fuck are they?"

Gunther shouted from the front stoop. "He texted a while ago, said there'd been a delay."

The three Lascos exchanged looks. The delay would be Stella. It felt like they'd spent half their lives waiting for her. Nate hated thinking how long his child's brain kept hoping his mother showing up was a good thing, and how crushing it was every time she reminded him he'd never have the warmth and approval he craved against his will.

Nate stalked back to the house and stopped in front of the stoop, arms crossed. He ignored the impression of a twenty-degree temperature drop in the shadow of the old house—the lack of sun accounted for it. "Can we at least go in there? Start setting up or whatever? I don't want to be here any longer than I have to."

Gunther shrugged, one hand shading his eyes. "I don't have the key. Helter wanted to make sure we got it on film—everyone going in for the first time, together. It's our standard opening."

Nate was hit anew with a jab of uneasiness, a feeling he'd made the wrong decision. He kept forgetting about the camera crew, though they were the reason for this family reunion. In his head, he pictured himself triumphant over a sobbing Stella, laying everything out, saying every word he'd left unsaid, letting her beg for once. He had a vague idea of getting a confession and using it to set things right, but whenever he remembered there would be real people behind the camera, strangers witnessing yet another Lasco family meltdown, he wondered what the hell he was doing here.

A text dinged from his pocket and he reached for his phone, brushing against the bottle of scotch. He considered finding a tree to duck behind and down some liquid courage, but the message on his screen was from Carrie.

*Remember to breathe. She can't hurt you anymore.*

He sighed and released his hold on the bottle in his pocket. In the years he'd known her, Carrie had become his safe place, the one person who kept him far enough from the edge that he wouldn't fall. Part of it was her—she had a knack for knowing what to say, and when he needed it. Another part was wanting to appear calm and stable for her. He craved her respect, her approval, though he tried not to think about what that implied about their relationship. Colleagues, that was all, and she'd never given any sign she wanted more. Still, he was grateful for what she did offer. The need to drink receded. It could wait until he'd done what he needed to do.

At long last a gold Hyundai Sonata pulled into the drive, crunching gravel as it went, stopping well clear of Gunther's bumper where Aury still sat.

Nate's mouth went dry, his heart thudding in his ears. He glanced at both his sisters; Katy pushing to her feet, hands clasped to stop them shaking, a painfully hopeful smile on her face, her breathing slightly labored until she took a pull from her inhaler. Aury on the bumper, only feet away from the Sonata, eyes still on the sky. She hadn't moved, and Nate hid a grin. She had her own armor against Stella, and he decided to follow her lead, turning his back on the car, studying the front windows of the house instead.

"Hey, guys, sorry to leave you hanging so long— Gunther been keeping you entertained?"

It was the host from the trailer; Nate recognized his voice. Helter. No one answered for a beat or two, until Katy giggled nervously.

"Of course, he's been great. Hardly noticed at all."

Someone cleared their throat and Nate listened to Helter scramble around the front of the car, uttering an apology as he opened the passenger door. Nate's body was strung tight, his nerves on edge, fighting the urge to turn around. He didn't want to give her the entrance she no doubt craved. A wave of acrid perfume washed over him, even ten feet from the car.

"Oh, my babies," came a soft, breathy voice. Nails on a chalkboard; he winced at the sound, at the stirring of resentment and anger it brought.

"Here all together, at long last. How I've dreamed of this day. Katy, sweetheart."

His youngest sister nearly leapt from the front porch, hurrying to her mother. "Good to see you, Mom," she said, her voice thick.

"Aury," Stella called next, her voice a caress. "Be a dear and get your mother's bags, will you?"

Aury didn't respond, and a quick glance over his shoulder showed Nate she still hadn't moved.

Stella sighed. "Nothing changes, does it? When you're done airdreaming, Aury, maybe you could listen."

"Oh. Hi, Mom."

A long silence stretched and Nate's nerves pulled taut, fighting an impulse to turn and run from this place. A slow crunch of gravel and another blast of that cloying perfume warned him of her approach, and still he didn't turn. Was he being petty, or adhering to the age-old wisdom of dealing with monsters? If you can't see them, they can't see you.

"My boy," she said in throbbing accents, stopping only a few feet away. "My *only* son. How good it is to see you."

Nate gritted his teeth. Only son? He reminded himself she was doing it on purpose, that this was how she operated. No matter how much he tried to prepare himself, she was always going to say something shitty he hadn't anticipated. He couldn't let it get to him.

Finally he turned, his expression stern, lips tight. He kept his hands in his pockets, and didn't move any closer to her.

"Stella."

If his use of her first name bothered her, she didn't show it. Instead she moved closer, reaching for his hands. When he didn't pull them out of his pockets, she settled for his wrists, holding him at an awkward angle, the missing weight of her left index and middle fingers like a phantom pain. He suddenly hoped Shawn *had* done it, that he'd gotten in a good hit before he died.

"My darling boy," she said in a low, breathy voice, and he wrinkled his nose at the sour, rotted stench of her breath. When was the last time she'd been to a dentist? He didn't want to look at her, but she wasn't letting go, so he finally lowered his gaze to meet hers.

She stared soulfully into his eyes for several seconds, then pressed his wrists. Once more, he could have sworn he felt all ten fingers.

"I want you to know, Nathan, that all is forgiven."

Nate frowned down at her, stumbled back a step. "What?"

She nodded and threw herself on his chest. "I forgive you, dear."

"You forgive *me?* What the fuck for?"

She stepped back without letting him go, smiled up at him. "Why, for destroying our family, my love."

# CHAPTER EIGHT

**IN THE RINGING** silence following Stella's words, all Nate could hear was the rush of blood in his ears underscoring the unbelieving vitriol that rose to his lips.

"Me? *I* destroyed our family?" He backed her up as he spoke, looming over her, reveling in every step she retreated. Fuck being prepared, taking the high road, controlling the narrative. He wanted her afraid. Nate had spent his life trying not to become his mother. He'd never been the kind of man people were afraid of, but in that moment, he wanted that to change. To be the kind of person whose very presence made others watch their tongues—he was sick of being the weak link. He quashed an uneasy feeling of deja vu, as though he were living out his terrible nightmares of the past week. But this didn't feel scary or bad or like he wasn't in control—he felt *alive*.

"Nate," squeaked Katy, but whatever else she said he tuned out. *Nate*, as though it were his fault instead of their mother's. If that's what she believed, then fuck her, too.

"I didn't destroy *shit*. I was the only one with the balls to stand up and say, enough. If I hadn't told the truth, how many of us would have survived childhood? You did it to Shawn, why wouldn't you do it to the rest of us?" Adrenaline rushed through his veins and he felt ten feet tall, ready to take on Stella, their father, and anyone else who'd made their lives a living hell.

Stella shook her head, lips trembling. "Are those the lies your father told you? And you believed him?"

49

"Nate," said Aury, at his shoulder without ever seeming to move. She touched him gently, not restraining him, just a little reminder she was there, and when she spoke, it was for his ears only. "She's not worth it. Don't let her do this to you. Not now."

It brought him up short, killed the rage, and shame rushed in to replace it. Only minutes in Stella's company and she'd already managed to overset him, knock him off his stride. That wasn't why he was here—no one ever listened to emotionally wrought people. It was an endlessly frustrating and unfair truth, one he'd seen play out over and over in his own clients when they tried to break their silence, to report the things someone they loved had done to them. The very fact of their visible pain made them unreliable, a little gauche. He looked up to see a camera pointed his way, resting on Helter's shoulder, the kid's face half hidden behind it.

"Turn that off," he snarled, but his anger had deserted him, left him sounding like a sulky teenager.

"Of course." Helter offered a smile, let the camera drop from his shoulder and turned to Gunther. "You gotta move faster than that, man," he said in a low voice. "That kinda shit is gold."

Rage flared again, but Aury's hand on his shoulder doused it once more. "Not worth it. This is what we're here for, remember?"

He turned, frowning. What the hell did that mean? They were here to be gaped at by film school rejects? He opened his mouth but she held his gaze, squeezed his arm hard, and let go.

"This is for us, not her. Remember that."

His mind was too scattered to make sense of her words or recall what she might be talking about, but he didn't get much chance to try.

"Nathan," began Stella, that nauseating note of authority in her voice. "I didn't come here to be talked to like that. I'm a victim, too—this thing, this haunting—I suffered more than anyone."

Nate's jaw dropped. "Really? You think you suffered more than Shawn? Because you're still here walking and talking, while my brother is fucking dead." The starkness of his words almost made him recoil. He'd never acclimated to the finality of Shawn's ending, to the cold reality of actual, literal death.

Stella pursed her lips in a smug little sneer. *I know something you don't know* it said, and Nate felt ten years old again. "You have no idea what happened that night. You weren't there."

"Who's fucking fault is that?" Nate said, his hands shaking.

She breathed in sharply through her nose. "Your brother was far from innocent. You've always idealized him, rewritten the past, but you know damn well what it was like living with someone that violent. It's important for all of us to accept our responsibility in the tragedy that befell our family."

By the time she finished her sentence, she was facing Helter, her chin lifted, expression just the right mix of wounded and strong. The camera, he reminded himself. All of it's for the camera. Don't feed into it. He ground his teeth and shoved his hands into his coat pockets, his fingers wrapping around both bottles of scotch. There if he needed them, whenever he needed them, and Carrie never had to know. He stared holes through Stella, daring her to keep pushing him, but with fresh meat in the form of Helter and Gunther, she'd forgotten Nate was there. The fight drained away, leaving him shaky and cold. He took a breath and went back to the SUV to gather himself, make sure none of the betraying tears that burned his eyes were allowed to fall.

"Whoa, whoa, whoa," said Helter, half laughing. "Come on back here, Nate. I know there's a lot of history here, a lot of emotions running high. That's great, that's the kind of stuff we need to work through today. But let's not forget, we're on the same side. We have a common enemy—don't let it divide us." He cast a glance back at the house, tossing hair out of his eyes.

Nate shook his head. "Jesus fucking Christ. You really buy into your own bullshit."

Katy started asking loud questions, trying to cover for his rudeness. Aury stayed silent, her eyes on the house, her shoulders hunched against the cold. What did she see when she fixed her gaze on the windows, when she peered around the side at the dilapidated shed that had housed their bikes and outdoor gear? Nate kept his focus on his sister while Stella made her way to Helter's side. In no time she was touching his shoulder, making eyes at him, and throwing her head back in fake laughter, a hand on her exposed cleavage. Helter laughed along with her as he and Gunther set up the shots, talked lighting and argued placements.

Nate pulled out his phone, wishing he had a best friend or a significant other to text. Give a play by play of the backwards reality he'd fallen into, letting someone else anchor him in truth with a series of *wtfs*. Instead he fell back on Carrie again, his only source of sanity that didn't come with a hangover.

*This is batshit.*

Several seconds went by, then the little ellipses appeared showing she was typing.

*Pretend you're on safari. Observe the wild animals in their natural habitat, safe in the knowledge you're going home after this.*

A brief pause, then:

*Stella's the baboon.*

Nate snorted and put his phone away, feeling calm again. He could do better than this. He *would* do better, so when he got his moment, when he was finally able to say what he needed to say, when he threw her into the limelight she thought she wanted, he'd be taken seriously. He had to keep his eyes on the prize, if he wanted her to suffer the way they'd all suffered. The way Shawn had suffered.

# THE DAY OF THE DOOR

Finding himself next to the overturned coffee cup in the front garden, he ducked down and pulled his brother's knife from the frozen ground. Ran his thumb against the cold blade, telling himself he was imagining the stickiness of dried blood. Tucked it in his right pocket where it clunked against the scotch.

There if he needed it, whenever he needed it. Just in case.

# CHAPTER NINE

**S**TELLA CLOSED HER EYES, pressed her palms together, breathed in deep. "He's here. I can feel him."

Candles flickered artfully on the dusty mantle behind her, casting her face in moving shadow. Though the production budget evidently ran to an expensive hired car, Gunther claimed not to have any ring lights, nothing that would soften the family's sharp edges. Nate hoped that meant Stella looked like shit on camera. Her vanity could stand a few knocks.

"Who?" he asked from his dark corner, tucked as far away from her as he could get. They gathered in the front room that opened onto the central staircase leading to the second floor. Everything so far looked much as he remembered, even some of the old furniture remaining, which surprised him. The wallpaper had faded and the whole place smelled faintly of must, but otherwise it was in good shape, especially for a house that had gone unoccupied for so long. It didn't feel like home, not by a long shot, but there were memories here, not all of them bad. He didn't know what he'd been expecting, but it wasn't this.

"Who, what, Nate?" asked Helter, one foot on the bottom stair, an arm cast over the railing.

"Who does she feel?" He refused to look at Stella.

"Him, of course," she said, her voice breathy and wounded. "Who else would you expect to find here?"

"But which him? Shawn? Or whatever the hell you're claiming did this to him? Who's here with us?"

The fragile facade dropped for a microsecond, the look she cast him pure fury, her lips pursed and trembling, on the verge of an outburst.

*Point one for Nate.*

It was Helter who answered, stepping once more into the breach. "Hey, let's do this thing in order, okay? We haven't reached the part about the entity yet, so let that be a reveal, m'man." The kid smiled and mimed clapping him on the shoulder from across the room, while Nate burned with the involuntary flush of shame at having screwed something up, missed the memo. Still, he'd gotten under Stella's skin, and that was a good thing.

*There's no shame in learning.* Another standard Carrie phrase, used to counter every apology he made for not already being perfect, for not getting it right the first time. The shame was a construct of his upbringing, no more. He still wished he could erase the knee-jerk pit in his stomach, the hot rush of embarrassment.

"Let's try this again, from the top. Ms. Lasco? Can you say that line one more time?"

Everyone went quiet, all eyes turned toward their mother. He could almost see her glow with the satisfaction of being the center of attention.

"I can feel him. He's here." She dropped her gaze and spoke directly to the camera. "My son is still in this house, waiting for me."

Aury's hand found Nate's wrist, pressed it tight, not looking at him. Words. They were only words.

"I, I think I feel him, too," said Katy in a breathless little voice. It made Nate shiver, look over his shoulder. He saw nothing.

Stella's face fell, her lips pursed once more when Gunther swung the camera toward her daughter.

"Tell us what you're feeling, Katy," said Helter, moving toward where she stood, neck craned to look up at the second-floor landing.

She laughed a little, but stopped when she encountered

her mother's glare. "Oh, I don't know. It just felt . . . kinda heavy in here? And I thought I smelled his body wash. It's stupid, don't listen to me. I probably imagined it."

"I smelled it, too," said Aury unexpectedly. "The stuff in that green bottle he used to douse himself with?"

Katy giggled and Nate found himself smiling. "Yeah, remember how it was like a cloud that followed him around? And no matter what we said, he wouldn't tone it down. Said it was a chick magnet."

For the space of a few seconds, Nate remembered his brother as he'd been, not as the tortured creature of his imaginings.

"What about you, Nate? You smell anything?" asked Helter, Gunther's camera turning his way.

Nate sniffed, grimaced, and raised his shoulders. All he smelled was must and Stella's overpowering perfume. "I don't think so." He met Katy's gaze, saw her face fall, and backpedaled. "I mean, maybe it was a little something—I didn't think about it at first, but yeah, there was definitely something there."

His little sister beamed at him, and he smiled back, her reassurance worth perjuring his soul. He didn't doubt she'd smelled it, maybe even Aury had, too. Nate wasn't a believer, not in ghosts or God, but for the first time he wondered if Shawn really might be here, haunting the place where he lost his life. He sure as shit hoped not—the single silver lining of his brother's death had been the comforting certainty that Shawn was finally safe from Stella's deft emotional torture.

"I've felt him so many times," intoned Stella, her voice louder, the drama ratcheted up to eleven. The camera swung back to her and she brushed hair behind her ears. "He comes to me."

"You're saying your eldest son, Shawn Lasco, who died in this house twenty years ago—he's been coming to you?" This from Helter, infusing his voice with over-the-top intensity.

Stella nodded solemnly. "Every night. That's why I knew it was time to come back, to face what really happened here. He's restless, and it's time to bring him peace."

"Where do you see him?" Nate couldn't help himself asking. "Have you been coming here?"

She turned her watery blue eyes on him. "No, he comes to me at home."

Aury spoke up, her gaze fixed on Stella. "What does he look like?"

Stella sniffed again, rubbed a tissue under her nose. "He looks perfect. Like he would have in life, if he wasn't so troubled."

Nate bit his lip hard enough to bleed, but Aury dropped her gaze, losing interest.

"He sits on the end of my bed and talks to me, every night. Tells me he's sorry." Her chin wobbled, perfectly timed tears spilling over her cheeks, tracking mascara in their wake.

"Oh, weird. So he hangs out at your place most of the time, but he's also been waiting around here for us to show up? Shawn gets around, I guess."

Gunther cut off a snort but Helter signaled for him to shut the camera off. He turned to Nate, his young face shaded with annoyance. "Nate, my guy, you gotta ease up on the sarcasm, okay? It's ruining the mood of the place. People tune in to see ghosts, and atmosphere. We want them to feel the fear we feel, to be in this with us, and that's not gonna happen with your quips."

Nate shrugged. "I figure they're also tuning in for family drama, right? Just giving the people what they want."

"Nathan Edward Lasco, stop trying to ruin everything *again*. You will do as you're told, do you understand me?" Stella's expression tightened his stomach, the look that had dominated his childhood, signaled things were about to go bad even if none of them understood why.

"Edwin," said Aury.

"What?" sputtered Stella.

"His middle name is Edwin, not Edward."

She gave her daughter a self-satisfied smile, one hand on her hip. "I think I remember what I named my own son. I was there."

"But she's right," said Nate. "It's Edwin."

Stella went still, her eyes emptying. Nate had the eerie feeling he was looking at an automaton powering down, or the dead eyes of a ventriloquist's dummy. Then she smiled again and tossed her hair. "Exactly what I said. Edwin. Told you, Aury, it's Edwin, not Edward. That kind of memory loss is concerning, honey. Does it happen a lot?"

"But you just—" Helter began, but Aury talked over him.

"Oh, my bad. Must have gotten confused." Aury's calm was unimpaired, glossing over the bizarre exchange.

Nate watched Helter staring at Aury, a frown on his face, which dispelled as soon as his sister turned her attention to him. A blush climbed the kid's neck and he cleared his throat.

"Listen, how about we cut to the chase here, Lascos. We can come back and shoot some of this stuff later, edit it in, no problems there. Right now, let's have it out. There's chairs in that extra sitting room on the second floor. You guys go on up, get settled, and we're gonna talk this through."

Nate swung his gaze to Stella, expecting her to protest, to draw things out. He knew she was fucking with them, had no intention of telling them what they so badly wanted to know, but when she nodded and started up the stairs, he couldn't stop his heart racing, his mouth going dry while his stomach did somersaults. Had she been telling the truth? Were they really going to get their questions answered? He fought hope at the same time dread trickled through his gut. Would he be able to handle knowing?

He flinched when Katy tucked her hand into his, her

fingers trembling in his grasp. He forced a smile. He was the eldest now, had been for a long time. He was no Shawn, but he could at least act like he was in control.

"You okay, kiddo? You look a little . . . wan, I guess." It was odd that he hadn't seen it at first, the exhaustion beneath her makeup, the worry pinching the corners of her eyes.

She looked away. "Of course, I'm great. Just haven't been sleeping so well."

He felt the smooth metal of her ring, a pinch in his palm where the stone pressed into it.

"Hey, congratulations on the engagement," he said, after confirming Stella was out of earshot.

Katy's cheeks reddened. "I'm sorry, I should have said something." She tried to smile. "I guess I was afraid of what you'd think."

"Because of the kids?" he asked.

"Yeah. Alexa and Zachary—they're wonderful. I wish you could meet them."

"I'd love to," he lied without hesitation. Giving her the answer he knew she wanted, instead of what he really thought. "They're going to be my niece and nephew, aren't they?"

Her shoulders sagged. "Maybe. I hope so. If things . . . work out."

Nate's gazed followed hers up the stairs in their mother's wake. All these years later, and the woman still kept them on a string, withholding any form of joy or source of happiness. Her face appeared over the railing on the second floor.

"Any time, kids. Let's get moving, shall we?"

Katy dropped his hand and started the climb. "Coming, Mom."

# CHAPTER TEN

"**A**LL THAT SUMMONING just to hurry up and wait," murmured Aury, leaning against the wall at the top of the stairs.

Nate tightened his arms around himself, trying and failing to smooth out his irritation at the delay. It was already the Stella show—she flitted around the central area where they were all meant to be sitting, asking Helter and Gunther to move this, push that over there, give her a seat with the best lighting. Katy accompanied her at first, sticking close and trying to help, but when Stella sighed audibly at her daughter's proximity for the fifth time, she retreated to where her brother and sister waited.

"She wants it to be perfect, I guess," said Katy in a small voice.

Nate frowned. Katy was shrinking into herself, the way she always did around Stella. He glanced around the room, his gaze falling on the dark hallway leading back to the upstairs bedrooms. Looking at it made his stomach flip. This whole place felt wrong, but how else would it feel?

"Looks like they're gonna be a while," he said, pushing off the wall. "Want to check out our old rooms? See what the new owners did with 'em?"

His sisters' response was halfhearted, and Nate wasn't excited at the prospect, either. But at least it was something to do beyond wait to be extras in the movie of Stella's life.

They fell in step, squeezing close to fit down the

hallway together, hovering shoulder to shoulder. No one was getting left behind this time. Not ever again.

Daylight from the front windows didn't penetrate more than a foot or two into the wood-paneled hall, and Nate slowed his steps, reluctant to cross into the shadowed land beyond. Had it always been this dark? He couldn't remember, his impressions of that time of his life jumbled by trauma. Even Aury hesitated, and Katy looked back the way they'd come. All at once Nate's certainties wavered at the heavy feel of the place. What if there *had* been something wrong here, beyond the family turmoil they'd lived with? What if his memories were real? Of Shawn disclosing something about a malevolent presence, telling him a dark secret he could no longer recall? He squinted into the darkness. Was there the outline of something that didn't belong?

Stella's shrill tones penetrated from the main room and when he looked again, the shadows were empty. As they'd always been. He set his jaw, taking Katy's hand once more. "C'mon. This one was yours, wasn't it? First door on the right?"

She gave a tiny nod and followed in his wake, drawing closer when the temperature dropped again. She shivered. "You guys feel that?"

"Colder," confirmed Aury from just over his shoulder. "By a few degrees, at least."

"It's just because sunlight can't get back here. The heat's not on, remember? It's bound to be colder."

They didn't argue, but no one breathed when he nudged open the grimy, once-white door to where the youngest of the Lascos used to sleep. The hinges swung slowly, creaking right on cue. Too bad Gunther wasn't here to catch it with his boom mic.

"Oh," said Katy, letting go of his hand and moving past him to be first into the room. She turned in a slow circle, not touching anything, her gaze traveling over the old canopy bed she'd had back then. Too small for her at that age, but she'd made the best of it.

Nate frowned and followed his sister in. "Was all this your stuff?" he asked, moving to the dresser that sat against the far wall. "This was yours too, wasn't it?"

Katy forced a laugh. "Yeah. I mean it could be—those things were probably mass-produced." Her gaze wandered over posters of horses and unicorns peeling from the plaster walls, the colors faded by time and dust. "This stuff wasn't mine. Maybe whoever bought it got the furniture with it, rented it furnished. We didn't take much with us, when we left." Her voice got small and her eyes glistened with threatened tears. Nate felt a lump in his own throat—she'd cried over that bed for months. Begged their father to get it for her, each time sunk into despair when he refused. Finally he'd told her the bed was gone, taken to the dump. She'd gotten as hysterical as Nate expected, and he shared her sense of loss, of wrongness that something she loved so much ended up in the trash heap.

"Furnished makes sense," Aury said flatly. "Might as well make use of what's there."

Nate glared at her, on the verge of reminding her she hadn't been there for Katy's breakdowns as a child. He stopped himself, sickened by the similarity to Stella's words. *You weren't there.*

"Wonder what else we left behind." Katy had stopped moving, standing beside the stripped bed, her eyes on the two folding closet doors. They were parted several inches, a deep darkness looking back at her, and she stepped closer to Nate.

A memory rose from the depths of his subconscious. Alien and completely unknown, yet with such force he didn't have the luxury of calling it false. Katy, breathless and wheezing, curled in a shivering ball in her bedclothes, pressed as close to the wall as she could get. Calling for her brother, for who knew how long—her voice never rose from a desperate whisper. He'd come running when he'd realized—hadn't he? Or was that Shawn? His memory declined to clarify, but he still saw the scene clear as day.

His little sister's eyes had been focused on the closet doors, and something that looked back at her with empty eyes. Nothing eyes, she'd said, and he shuddered.

Katy took his arm and held it tight, her proximity meaning he could hear the wheeze of her lungs closing. His own chest tightened in sympathy.

"Your inhaler," he said, speaking as softly as she did. "Where is it?"

She gave no sign of having heard, her gaze still caught by that sliver of darkness. Of course there was nothing there—how could there be? So why was that harder to believe, the longer he stared? Was that a profile? A dirty white t-shirt below a shadowed face with nothing eyes? Hairs rose on the back of his neck and cold washed over him.

"Do you see it?" Katy whispered.

Aury saved him the trouble of answering. She moved past her siblings, lifted one foot and delivered a punishing kick to the closet doors, slamming them closed. Dust and dead insects exploded into the air, filling what little light there was with swirling motes.

"Doesn't fucking matter," she said, her upper lip lifted in something close to a snarl. "Come on. Let's get out of here."

Katy transferred her grip to her sister's hand and they hurried to the door, Nate following in their wake. He couldn't stop himself from turning to look, one last time, and when he did his breath caught.

Something leaned in the corner of Katy's bed, the same place she'd cowered as a small child, afraid of monsters in the closet. It blended with the dark so well Nate could easily have talked himself out of acknowledging it, if it weren't for the teeth. Two rows, top and bottom, far too long for this reality, dully gleaming from the shadows with nothing above them. A gap between the rows as though something with hungry jaws watched him. Waiting to pull him close and swallow him whole.

# CHAPTER ELEVEN

**THEY SAT IN** a semi-circle of plush leather chairs. The furniture smelled new, but was butter soft, the leather already broken in for maximum comfort. Those chairs should have looked out of place in the grimy house, but the second-floor sitting room was in better shape than the downstairs and the bedrooms, the cobwebs and dust gone, the floor polished to a dull glow. Whatever Gunther claimed about no one entering the house until the cameras were rolling, someone clearly had. The setting grounded Nate, took him away from the place where he was still a scared teenage boy. These were set pieces, because this whole thing was a farce. Here on stage with the other actors, he could convince himself he hadn't seen anything in Katy's room. None of them had, because ghosts weren't real.

His heart rate nearly normal, he ran a hand over the back of one chair and gave a low whistle. "Not bad."

"You're welcome," said Aury over his shoulder, once again soft enough that no one else heard. He raised an eyebrow and smiled—she'd said this was for them, hinted at plans of her own. He realized she hadn't reacted much to the creepy bedroom and relief flooded his body. The situation was controlled—it was only the emotional residue left in this place making him see things. Everything else, everything tangible, was orchestrated by Aury, or The Cleaners. He couldn't even be mad about it—whatever unease he'd felt would be worth sticking it to Stella. He didn't like scaring Katy, though—he'd talk to Aury about bringing their sister in on the secret. For now he sat between his siblings and took a deep breath. He could do this.

At the center of the horseshoe of chairs was Stella, sitting primly on the edge of her seat, one leg crossed over the other at the ankle, poised in the most flattering position she could muster. She looked into the camera Gunther had set on a stand in the center of the group.

"My name is Stella Lasco, and for the past twenty years, I've been battling demons."

Nate rolled his eyes. Oh, so now they weren't just ghosts, but demons. They'd upgraded in the last half hour.

"Things weren't always like this," she said, her voice going husky. "Before we moved here to the Harper Lane Hell House—"

Nate smothered a snort, and he wasn't the only one, though he couldn't be sure who else had been overcome.

Stella's eyes flicked to his face and away again, and he tried not to feel wilted by the disgust in her gaze. When she spoke again it was with a raised voice that echoed against the high ceilings. Nate fought a surge of anxiety. His body remembered all too well what that tone entailed, his brain dumping adrenaline into his blood, telling him to move, get the fuck out. Instead he held himself still, counted his breaths in and out. This wasn't the time to lose it.

"Before we moved here, I had an ideal family life. I was a loving wife, a doting mother to my children. I gave them everything." Nate clenched his jaw, remembering overdrawn school lunch balances, red-stamped utility bills. No dental visits after the divorce, no eye doctors though he'd been placed in the front row of every classroom, squinting at the squiggles on the chalkboard. Yet somehow there was money for weekly mani pedis, luxury hotel stays, expensive clothes. *I deserve it* was what she'd always said.

"It was hard, but I live for my family, so I didn't mind the sacrifices I made for them."

*For us, or of us?* Nate wanted to ask.

"Tell us how it started," said Helter, as Gunther panned the camera from face to face. Nate could only be grateful to him for breaking into what promised to be a long and nauseating self-congratulatory soliloquy.

Stella blew out a breath, smoothed her hands over her slacks. "I've never had an easy life, Helter," she began, before he stopped her.

"Don't talk to me, talk to the camera. We're bringing the audience along with us, so speak to them directly. Really make them feel it—this is your big chance to tell your side."

She froze, her carefully crafted expression crystallizing into something brittle. "What's that supposed to mean? My *side*? You asked me to come here to tell what happened—there aren't any sides here. Only the truth."

Nate flinched involuntarily at the bite in her voice, the rising note of anger that signaled a coming storm. He didn't much like Helter, but he felt an urge to pull the kid out of harm's way. *A safari. Only a safari—I get to go home after this.*

Helter didn't seem daunted. "Of course. I just meant, you haven't talked publicly before about what happened that day. Please, go on."

Her dead-eyed stare stayed fixed on his face for several uncomfortable seconds before she remembered to slide her human mask back in place. "Yes, of course. Anyway, as I was saying, things were great for a long time. I was able to provide my kids with every advantage, an idyllic childhood, really. That all changed once we came here."

*Idyllic, my ass.*

"And what prompted the move?" Helter asked.

"It was after my husband left me." Her tone dipped, ended on a strained note. "Left me like trash on the side of the road, and the kids, too. He never loved them—they all know that. He used them as a way to trap me."

She didn't bother looking at her children while she

made her breezy declaration. Nate felt that familiar slip of reality, the slide into a world of Stella's own creation that bore no resemblance to his memories or truth.

"So there I was, a single mother with four kids and no child support, no roof to keep over their heads."

"That's really odd, isn't it?" asked Helter, once more interrupting her flow.

"What is?" she asked in a voice like broken glass.

"Well, that he'd take off like that, not provide any support at all. And the courts wouldn't assign child support, or give you the house, since you had custody of the kids?"

Nate smiled. Maybe this Helter kid was okay.

Stella passed a shaking hand over her face, the one with the missing fingers. "It's all so hazy by now, and I had no one to help me. I was on my own—I've never had anyone to turn to. I haven't been myself since all of this happened, but I know he lied on the stand, their father. Convinced the judge I wasn't a fit parent—I had to sign away any alimony, child support or interest in the house just to keep my babies."

Nate frowned. This was new information, and thus highly suspect. Stella loved nothing better than to live over and over all the incidents of cruelty, all the people who tried to screw her over, and the times she triumphed over them. If this shit had happened back then, they'd have already heard the story twenty times.

"I see. Certainly an upsetting turn of events. So how did you get hold of this house? It's pretty spacious—had to be pricey, even twenty years ago."

"What's your point?" Stella asked, the hostility as sudden as a snake bite.

Helter smiled, raised a hand. "Only that it's really impressive. You taking care of all four kids on your own, no help at all, and you manage to land this place. Plenty of room for everyone, that kind of thing. You really stepped up."

*Nice save.*

She relaxed, the waxen smile melting back in place. "Yes, of course. You're right on the money. It wasn't easy, but I wanted them to have the best of everything, even if I went without." Tears gathered again. "I thought I was doing the right thing, but from the first day, I felt the darkness here."

"Tell us about that."

Stella eased back in her seat. "It was a feeling of oppression, the second I walked in the door. I was carrying a box and all at once it was too heavy for me, like the weight of the world was on my shoulders. It felt like hands pushing me down, but there was no one here."

"And was that the only time you felt that weight?"

"No, of course not. It was only the beginning. After that, I started noticing things going missing, doors opening on their own. Footsteps on the third floor keeping me awake at night. And always, always that heavy shadow." She shuddered.

Nate frowned, his hind brain stirred by her mention of a shadow. The image was muddled, but he saw himself in the scratchy playback of childhood, standing in a kitchen and watching Stella's shadow precede her into the room. In his mind, the shadow slunk, moving independently of the woman who cast it. And when it crept about the house at night, its footsteps echoed.

He cast aside an image of shivering on his childhood bed, head beneath the blankets, breath held as he listened. Shadows don't make noise. He didn't need paranormal explanations to know what paced ominously in the hall outside his room,

Helter appeared unimpressed with her story. That made sense—the guy hosted a ghost-hunting show, so this kind of thing was run of the mill. "Did you have any sense of what it was, what it might be tied to? Something from your past, maybe?"

She pursed her lips. "From the past, yes, but not *my* past."

Helter frowned. "What do you mean by that?"

She lifted her chin, gave an arch smile. "This place has seen darkness before."

Helter looked at Gunther, who shrugged. He turned his attention back to Stella. "I'm not sure I understand. We never turned up anything in our research, nothing that predates when you moved in."

Her smile was infuriatingly smug. "You'd have to know where to look."

"Uh, okay, so can you tell us about that? What did you find out about the house?"

"All in good time," she said. "All you need to know for now is I'm telling the truth. There's something here, something old, and I felt it from the very first day."

Nate rolled his eyes. More bullshit. If the place had some kind of lascivious history, she'd have told them all about it. She wouldn't go into it because it was completely fabricated.

"Okay, let's go back to that, then. When you felt this darkness, did you talk to anyone about it? The kids, or another adult?"

Stella cast her eyes down. "Who would I talk to? I had no one, and I didn't want to frighten the kids. Not when we'd all been through so much already."

"So at what point did you tell your brother about it? Was that later?"

She pursed her lips, flustered. "Ron? No, I never told him anything. He never knew, and he wouldn't have cared if he did."

"Really. Even though he was the one footing the bill for the house?"

Nate frowned, glanced at Katy, then Aury, but neither were looking at him. This was the first he'd heard of Uncle Ron contributing anything to their family—he'd ostensibly washed his hands of his younger sister when Shawn and Nate were little. Reading between the lines of Stella's diatribes, Ron didn't much care for kids, or his sister, and given his staunchly conservative stances, he'd probably disapproved of the divorce. So why would he have helped with living expenses? Maybe money was just the easiest option to get her off his back.

Stella sputtered. "He did *not*, that's not how it was. I had no one, why can't you understand that?'

Helter nodded. "Yes, sorry, go on, please. You mentioned before some kind of a visitation, right? What happened, exactly?"

Stella wrapped her arms around herself. "I wasn't sleeping well. I haven't for years—too much to worry about. But one night I felt a weight on my bed, and I couldn't move."

"That's creepy," said the host, leaning in closer. Here, finally, was where things might get juicy.

"It was. I looked up, and I just *knew* something was there, standing over me. I could feel it back there, and smell it, too."

"You smelled it?"

She wrinkled her nose. "Yes. Its skin smelled . . . rancid. And it had these eyes—they were the only thing I could see, these two glowing blue eyes in the darkness."

Nate's heart lurched and his face went cold, her description too close for comfort. The glowing blue eyes from his dream—did that mean he'd actually seen them? Had Shawn?

"And was it after that when you started noticing changes in your behavior?"

Her cheeks flushed red. "I'm . . . I'm not certain. I think whatever happened, it's affected my memory."

"But there *were* changes, right? Stuff that was out of character?"

Stella's hands trembled. "Small things, yes, but I don't recall exactly—"

"Makes sense. That's why we have the whole family here, right?" Helter made a twirling movement with one finger and Gunther panned the camera. "Why don't you kids tell us how things changed, what you remember from that time? Katy, you want to start?"

Katy cast frantic glances between her mother and the camera, her nails digging into the arms of her chair. "Oh, I don't, um, I'm not sure I'm the best person to . . . " She trailed off, looked at Nate.

He took a breath and sat forward, pushing aside the queasiness, his doubts. Now was the time, his chance to get it all out there. Do what he came here to do, and reclaim his life. He opened his mouth but before he could speak, Aury filled the silence.

"I remember mood changes." She didn't look at the camera, but at Stella. "It was really erratic—you'd be fine one minute, then the next blowing up at one of us. We never knew what to expect."

Stella broke in, speaking through clenched teeth. "That's simply untrue. I'm about as patient as anyone could be, with four kids on my hands—"

Helter put a hand up. "Let's hear from Aury now. This happens a lot, families remembering things differently, which is why it's important to let everyone speak." He didn't give Stella a chance to reply, but turned back to Aury, his voice noticeably warmer, that light flush climbing his neck again. Nate narrowed his eyes. Did the kid have a crush? "You can go on. What else do you remember?"

"The mood swings were bad, because they were unpredictable." Aury's voice never changed, every word delivered in that same flat, emotionless way. "We never knew what would set you off, so we were always on edge. One second I'd be doing my chores, vacuuming with my headphones in, then you'd be in my face screaming about stuff that made no sense. You were pretty unhinged."

Stella looked ready to explode, her face bright red, jaw clenched and trembling, but Helter spoke before she could.

"Wow, that's intense. So that argues something pretty powerful had hold, huh?" The camera turned back to Stella, who gave a thin, hard smile.

71

"Yes, yes it did. That's the only thing that could make me treat my children like she's saying. Though I think it's very possible whatever it was interfered with their memories as well."

"Hmm, sure, that's a theory. So what about physical violence?"

Stella started to answer but Aury mowed right over her. "Yes. Not over the top by some standards—there was a lot of slapping, backhands, some hair pulling. Things like that. But it was worse for Shawn."

"How so?" asked Helter.

Nate looked from his sister to his mother, his mouth dry, heart pounding. He couldn't believe this was finally happening, on camera no less, and he hadn't even had to open his mouth. He felt a prick of guilt, letting Aury take the fall, but he wasn't about to stop this train derailing.

"That's the point, we don't really know." She still spoke directly to Stella, her gaze unwavering, though her mother was unable to hold her eyes. The older woman's lips moved, muttering something low through clenched teeth, but Aury took no notice. "You'd drag him behind closed doors—you did it to all of us. Pull one from the herd and leave the rest of us listening and scared. It happened most often to Shawn. He never talked about what happened." Her voice lowered. "Not to me, anyway."

Nate's memory conjured an image of his older brother, crying with his teeth clenched, his eyes reddened and narrow. The slam of Shawn's door in Nate's face—the Lascos had definitely bought into the whole boys don't cry, toxic masculinity bullshit. Had he ever asked what went on beyond the door? He couldn't recall, and when he thought of the times he'd been dragged there, his shoulder aching, wrist twisted in Stella's sweaty hold, the memory always ended in a blank, dark surface.

He felt sick, momentarily robbed of speech. Repressed memories—that was new. He'd thought everything about childhood was burned ineradicably into his psyche. They might be false—memories were tricky and unreliable. But it *felt* real. As real as the day Shawn died, that same fury in his face, even after Stella hit him.

It had shocked them all into silence, breath frozen in their chests as they felt the world tilt beneath their feet. They'd adapted to life as they knew it, dealt with the slaps and other cruelties so common in that era, knowing plenty of kids had it worse. But she'd crossed a line that day, bringing the metal bat with her. Nate remembered staring at it, thinking it was only for show. Surely Stella wouldn't actually hit any of them with it. But then he'd seen that empty, dead-eyed stare, and he knew there would be no reasoning with her. Mom's gone, kids, no one's home. The solid and sickening thunk of the baseball bat connecting with Shawn's forehead, Stella moving so fast none of them saw it coming. Blood trickling from his brow into his eyes, a goose egg rising in the wake of Stella's blow. Nate shuddered. Knowing what he did now about head injuries, he wondered if Shawn would have lived through that day regardless of what happened behind the door.

Stella sat forward, rage making her whole body tremble. "I did *nothing* to you children you didn't deserve," she hissed in accents of loathing. Before she could keep going, Katy spoke up as though she hadn't heard her mother.

"I . . . I remember the lies," she said in a small, breathless voice.

Gunther made a wide swing of the camera on its stand and Katy blushed, shrunk into her chair.

"Excuse me, young lady?" Stella said.

Katy licked her lips, her eyes darting. "No, see that's what I'm saying, Mom. It makes sense that it was something else controlling you, because it was so awful, and it wasn't like that before. Was it?" She fixed a pleading gaze on her mother's face, and Nate's heart sunk. She so badly needed to believe the fairy tale of Stella's making. But even now, Stella withheld that crumb of comfort, her cold gaze and twisted lips the only answer her daughter would get.

"Tell us about the lies, Katy," said Helter.

Katy broke away from Stella's gaze, wrapped her arms around herself. Gunther smiled encouragingly from behind the camera. "It was weird stuff. Like saying she'd paid a bill for school when she hadn't, or blaming stuff on us when it obviously wasn't true. Telling us we did things on purpose to hurt her, like by forgetting to unload the dishwasher, we were conspiring to make her life hard."

Her words brought another wave of sense memory to Nate, of staring at his mother open-mouthed, unable to defend himself against accusations of motivations that had never crossed his young mind. He thought he'd dealt with all of this, faced the worst and moved on from it. How much more had his mind simply rejected?

Katy kept going, fixated on Gunther like he was her lifeline. "And the worst part was when we'd try to reason with her, show her notes from the guidance counselor, or tell our side of something, and she'd just purse her mouth and give us this empty stare like we weren't even there."

Nate glanced at Stella, meeting that same empty stare. *Nothing eyes.* His stomach flipped. He remembered it now, too. The way she'd look through him when he spoke, like he didn't exist to her.

"Nate? Let's hear from you, now. What do you remember most about how things changed when you moved into the house?"

Nate's face went cold and he stared blankly at the camera, opening and closing his mouth. What happened to his words? All the things he'd promised himself he'd say to her, the truths he'd finally speak, the answers he'd demand? All of it was gone, vanished from his mind, eclipsed by a store of memories finally finding their way into the light. He stayed frozen for a beat, then straightened. Getting his licks in was less important than what he could do for his sisters.

"I remember all of that," he said hoarsely. "Everything you both said. The moods, isolating us from each other. Lying while she looked right through us." He took a breath, met Stella's gaze. "Lying about the abuse."

There it was. The 'a' word, never spoken between them, a label never applied because back then it had seemed so *big*, too big for what was happening in their little family. Abuse was much worse than what they'd experienced, wasn't it? It could always get worse. They knew because Stella told them so.

Helter nodded like he'd done something right, and Aury gave him the tiniest of smiles.

"Stella?" said Helter, breaking the silence before it could smother them. "Want to tell us how all that felt to you when you were going through it?"

The silence drew out while she sat and glared at each of them in turn, hatred distorting her features, a promise of retribution to come. Nate had to remind himself there was nothing she could do to him—not anymore. It still couldn't kill the dread.

With visible effort Stella pulled herself together and faced the camera. "As I said, I believe *all* of our memories were affected by the . . . phenomena present in this house. And of course teenagers lie, especially mine." She gave a brittle laugh. "So *inventive*. But in any case, I can assure you that however bad it might have been for you kids . . . " She paused, let the fury with which she'd spat 'kids' echo through the room. "However bad you *think* you had it, it was far, far worse for me."

Nate thought he might chew through his own tongue, he was biting it so hard. *I, me, my, mine.* The language of her people.

Helter nodded sympathetically. "Tell us about that."

Stella preened a bit, happy in the spotlight once more, ready to hold forth at length about her sufferings. "No one will *ever* know how hard I fought. It was *agony*, sheer *agony* every minute of every day, but I had to protect my kids, no matter the cost to myself."

Nate frowned, tilting his head to the right, trying to pick out a new sound beneath the grating of her voice. It was low, almost a scraping, quiet enough he couldn't be sure it was even there. "Anyone else hear that?" he asked.

Stella looked at him coldly. "I'd like to ask that you all stop interrupting me. It's really hard to keep the flow of the narrative."

*Or keep your lies in order*. He raised his hands. "Fine."

She narrowed her gaze. "Fine, what?"

"Fine . . . Stella?"

"You know that's not—"

"Shh, I hear it too," said Aury, cutting in on her mother. "What the hell is that?"

Gunther frowned and glanced over his shoulder, to where the staircase rose into darkness. Then he looked back at the viewscreen of the camera and fiddled with settings.

"There's definitely something. The equipment's picking it up, too."

Helter stood and jogged to his side, peering over the bigger man's shoulder. "Are we set up for EVP?"

"I mean, anything the mics pick up we can go back and enhance . . . " said Gunther uneasily, with another look at the staircase.

"I hear it, too," announced Stella, her voice louder than necessary. She sat ramrod straight in her chair, hands clutching the soft, rounded arms of it. She closed her eyes and breathed deep. "It's him. He's talking to me."

Nate stood and moved closer to the stairs, his heart hammering. "That's not what I'm hearing—it's not a voice. It's like a . . . I don't know, kind of a dragging maybe?" His mouth was dry, throat aching. It was the sound from his dream, the dream that seemed more real every minute he spent in this house. He turned to Aury, still frozen in her chair. "Is that what you hear?"

She nodded, and so did Gunther.

Katy frowned and got up to stand next to her brother,

casting a wary glance up the dark stairs. "I hear it, now. It's kind of . . . rhythmic, whatever it is." She wrapped her arms around herself and Nate saw that she was shaking. "It sounds . . . familiar, but I don't think . . . "

Stella licked her lips, her eyes darting from side to side, her hands shaking. "Yes, of course, and I know what it is. It's your poor brother, pacing those halls over and over."

Even Helter waved Stella off this time. "No, that's not it. Nate's right, it's . . . man, I don't know. It's kind of a dragging across a hard surface."

Nate nodded, snapping his fingers. "Yeah, yeah that's exactly it. Like something metal, maybe."

"We need to leave," said Aury, pushing out of her chair. The color drained from her face and her hands shook at her sides.

"Aury?" he said. He couldn't remember the last time she'd looked that scared.

Helter got to her before Nate could. He reached for Aury, took hold of her wrist. "It's okay. This is what we came for, remember?"

Aury yanked her hand away, her brows snapping together. "I can't," she said tightly. "I didn't think it would happen like this, so fast, and—"

The sound grew louder, drowning out her words. The endless drag of metal along wood, closer with every step, yet nothing appeared.

Katy said it was familiar, he reminded himself. Whatever it was, it hadn't originated in Nate's dream, but was instead something they'd experienced together. He'd probably just forgotten, the way he'd forgotten all the other things his sisters remembered.

He looked at Aury, brows drawn, but she shook her head. "I don't know where it's coming from," she said softly, her teeth chattering. "We need to go, now."

If nothing else convinced him, that certainly did, and he knew he should leave, lead them out before anything else happened. But he couldn't let go of it, couldn't walk away without knowing. The sound kept getting louder, and Nate's skin prickled, his shoulders hunched against a sudden drop in temperature.

"What the fuck . . . " breathed Gunther, brandishing a handheld instrument he'd fished out of a bag at his feet. It made frantic clicking noises, ramping up in tandem with Nate's fear. He turned wide eyes to Helter, then gestured up the stairs to the third floor. "Man, maybe we should turn that thing off."

Helter scowled at him, made a slicing movement across his throat.

Nate frowned. "What are you—" he began to ask, but got no further.

"What is it, what the hell is it?" yelled Katy, clapping her hands over her ears, tears spilling from her bright eyes.

He knew he should stop and comfort her. Shawn would have done so, no matter what else was going on. But the sound . . . it kept going, the volume increasing until the whole house shuddered with it. Whatever made that noise, it was at the top of the stairs, where Gunther had indicated. Maybe the ghost hunters knew something, had sensed or saw something they hadn't shared. He should check it out. Go up to the third floor, the place where his brother lost his life. Nate felt summoned, pulled. He needed to get up there, climb all the way to the top and see what he was supposed to see. What his mind was protecting him from.

Terror should have held him in place—he'd never been the adventurous one, always opting out of the fun things the others did without thought. Water skiing, tubing, horseback riding, back when Dad was still around and that kind of thing happened from time to time. He was the only Lasco born without a daredevil streak, but today his feet moved without him. Whatever the sound was, it had something to do with Shawn. The dead boy wanted his brother to ascend, to see, acknowledge his pain. This might be his last chance.

"Nate, don't," Katy called, yelling to be heard above the scraping sound resonating through their bones. She grabbed at his arm but he pulled away, intent on answering the call.

"I don't know if I would," yelled Gunther as he passed, but Nate ignored him, too.

At the top of the stairs, hidden in darkness and drifting dust particles, a shadow loomed. Someone was up there, just out of sight, unnaturally still.

Nate stopped at the bottom of the second staircase, one hand on the banister, a foot on the first step. "Shawn?" he said softly, hoping like hell it wasn't him. That whatever made that tortured noise, whatever stood eyeless in the dark had nothing to do with his big brother. He looked at the next step, unable to make himself move.

The sound increased, the house rocking with its intensity. Nate looked over his shoulder at Aury standing next to her chair with her eyes closed, hands pressed over her ears, Helter hovering nearby. Stella was nowhere in sight, but he couldn't stop to find her. He sensed his window closing, and he needed to know.

"Shawn!" he called, and began to climb. Just as his foot hit the third stair, the sound cut off abruptly, the tension in the air snapping like a wire. The silence was oppressive, as heavy as the noise had been, then in the hush of perfect quiet, something thudded onto the stairs from above. Two somethings, lightweight, spinning end over end, bouncing on each step while Nate watched, trying like hell to place what he was seeing.

They stopped on the third step, lodged against his shoe, and he leaned close, squinting in the gloom, then rearing back when he realized what they were.

An index and middle finger, sawed at the joint, dried, ragged flesh sticking out in a nauseating fringe, each nail painted a bright, vibrant red. As Nate watched, the index finger uncurled from itself, pointed directly at him, then bent inward.

Beckoning. Calling. Hooking him into whatever was taking place in this hellhole.

A scream erupted from behind him, then a heavier series of thuds, with a sickening crunch at the bottom. Nate ran to peer over the second story landing and saw Stella, crumpled far below, staring up at him, blood trickling from the corner of her mouth.

# CHAPTER TWELVE

"**WELL, SHE'S NOT DEAD,**" said Aury, settling into the backseat of Gunther's SUV.

"Fuck."

"Nathan!" said Katy, her emotions overwrought. "How can you? I know she's not been the most loving mom, but you'd feel terrible if she really did die."

It wasn't the first time he'd been hit with that statement, and he didn't bother to argue with her. He'd spent a lot of time processing the fucked-up nature of his childhood, giving himself room to feel his feelings, and was fairly certain that when the day finally came, when someone called to tell him Stella was dead, he'd feel nothing.

Except that wasn't quite true. For when he'd looked over that railing, seen his mother lying there, apparently sightless and motionless, he'd felt only a flood of blissful relief, followed immediately by a stab of intense annoyance. Of course she'd die now, right when she'd convinced all of them she was going to tell them the truth about Shawn's death. That figured.

He refused to acknowledge the other thing he'd seen, tucked in shadows beside the staircase. There was nothing there, just as there'd been nothing in Katy's closet. Unless it was something Aury orchestrated, as a way to scare Stella into submission. Gunther had said something about "turning that thing off"—he must have been talking about a projector of some kind, or whatever could create an image like that. His gaze fell on his sister, settling into the more palatable explanation.

Aury smiled without opening her eyes and he fought a confusing mix of relief and irritation at her. Of course she'd done it—he was starting to think she'd done all of this. He had to hand it to her, that performance back at the house had scared him good. Who knew she was such a talented actress?

"Katy, people process things differently. We see it all the time. It doesn't make your brother a bad person—let him feel what he feels, okay?"

Nate's stomach dipped, recalling Gunther's presence with a start. They'd all been treating him like so much furniture in the mad dash to the hospital in the wake of the ambulance, and it was jarring, remembering he was a living, breathing human who'd heard every unguarded thing that fell out of their mouths.

"Should I . . . should someone go up there? To be with her, I mean?" asked Katy.

Aury shrugged. "Helter's out in the hall. He said he'll text when she wakes up."

An odd set-up if Nate ever heard one—all three of Stella's remaining children hiding out in the parking lot while a kid they barely knew stood vigil. They all felt it, tinged with varying degrees of guilt, but none were keen on leaving the comfort of the vehicle, so Helter it would be. Fuck it. Let him earn his ratings.

"So what now?" Nate asked. "I mean, is that it? Is it over?"

Gunther shrugged, but Aury shook her head, her jaw set. "No. It isn't over, because we didn't get what we came for. I want answers, and I'm not giving up until we get them."

Nate frowned. "Aury, seriously. This has gone far enough, don't you think?"

Gunther cleared his throat and popped the driver's door open. "I'm gonna go grab a coffee from the gas station." He set off into the cold and Nate found himself really liking the guy. He didn't seem to have kids, either, so maybe Katy could marry him, instead.

Katy caught her breath on a sob. "I'm not sure I can go back there," she said in a low voice. "I mean, that was really scary, right? My old room, the closet. And whatever the hell that other thing was, that noise . . . "

"You said it sounded familiar. It did to me, too."

Her gaze darted to his, her mouth falling open. "You've heard it?"

He nodded and ducked his head, frowning down at his lap. "Matter of fact, it freaked me out at first because I could've sworn it came from a dream. But then you said you remembered it and I realized we must've heard it when we were kids."

She leaned closer, her voice dropping. "You've been having bad dreams?"

He shuddered. "The fucking worst. Ever since I agreed to do this stupid show."

She bobbed her head in three quick nods. "It's been awful—they all start with that damn sound, and even if my lungs are fine, a few seconds listening to that and I feel like I'm suffocating. I don't know why, but it's like it . . . triggers something."

Nate took a purposefully deep breath, trying to calm his own triggered psyche. "And do you feel . . . anything? See anything?"

She frowned. "Maybe—I can't remember, exactly. There's something there with me, though. Something that's already in the bed—I feel it moving beside me, all around me, and when I try to get away, it . . . it—" She shuddered, dropped her voice. "Whatever it was, it crawled *inside* me, and then every night after that I've dreamed of . . . " She trailed off, rubbed her hands over her arms and looked away. "Never mind. Bad stuff."

Nate's heart thudded in his ears. "Bad stuff like *doing* bad things to people?"

Tears welled up again in her eyes and her lips trembled, her cheeks flushed like she was ashamed. "To Tim, sometimes. I dream I literally bite his head off. He makes me mad, so I . . . like, unhinge my jaw and everything, and I have all these horrible teeth and my hands don't look right, they're like, ugh." She shuddered, tucking her hands under her arms. "But the worst part is the kids," she whispered hoarsely. "I dream I'm screaming at them or slapping them, driving off and leaving them alone." She swallowed hard. "And . . . other stuff. Worse than that. Bad enough that when I wake up I feel guilty, almost afraid to talk to them at all. Tim's even noticed—he asked me yesterday if I was having second thoughts about getting married." Her voice broke on the last word and she buried her face in her hands.

"And are you?" he asked, feeling like an asshole. "Having second thoughts, I mean."

Aury glared. "Nate. Shut the fuck up."

Katy raised her eyes, tears streaming down her face. "Of course I've had second thoughts—and third, and fourth, and fifth. I worry about the same shit you do, that I'm gonna fuck it up. That I'll become *her*, whether I want to or not. I've told Tim a hundred times, but he just doesn't get it. He never lived like we did, so he thinks it's jitters." Her chin trembled. "I know what we promised. I know I should walk away—it's what I've always done in the past. Or I would have, if anyone ever stuck around long enough for it to be my choice." She gave a broken laugh. "But Tim . . . he's different. He's like no one I've ever known, let alone dated, and I just want . . . I want to be happy."

Nate knew she wanted his blessing, his absolution. Though it wasn't up to him, he knew he should give it to her. It was normal for their generation to need validation from outside themselves, and the Lasco kids more than most. They'd never gotten it at home, so they'd all sought it in different ways, with varying measures of success, since they'd flown the coop. Nate drank, and buried himself in work, and waited like a stupid puppy for Carrie's approval, he thought bitterly. Aury convinced herself and everyone else she was an island, that she didn't need anyone or anything. And Katy . . . Nate watched her tear-streaked face. Katy had sought it from every man who crossed her path, who showed her even a crumb of attention.

Aury leveled a look at him, then lowered her sunglasses and took her sister's hand. "You're not her, okay? None of us are. Her sins aren't ours, and you *deserve* to be happy. You're going to get married, and look sickeningly gorgeous in a sparkly gown, and be an awesome mom to those kids. Dreams are just that—dreams. They don't reflect anything but your own worries." She turned her gaze on her brother. "You should know that better than anyone, Dr. Freud."

He looked back at her steadily. "What about you, Aury? Any nightmares?"

She nudged her shades back up her nose. "Not a one. That's not surprising—I never dream. Not that I remember, anyway."

Nate fought a surge of jealousy. Oh, to be Aury, and have the ability to shut it all off. Stop feeling, stop thinking, stop dreaming. Stop all the fucking suffering. He took a breath and tamped down his jealousy.

"I think the house really is haunted," said Katy in a small voice. "All those meters and stuff going off, and the way that sound started from nowhere and got so loud." She put her hands over her ears. "It reminded me . . . it made me think of Mom."

Nate patted her leg. "It scared me too, but we'll find an explanation." He leveled a gaze at Aury, but she stared right back.

"I told you in there. It wasn't me."

Katy lowered her hands. "How could it be you?"

Aury pursed her lips. "I just said it wasn't."

Katy transferred her gaze to Nate. "Then why . . . "

Nate sighed. "Aury, seriously? I don't care what you do to Stella—you can funhouse scare her to death if you want.

A well-timed heart attack would solve a lot of problems for all of us. But you need to stop scaring Katy. It's not fair."

Aury sat up, her mouth twisting. "I'm not. I fucking told you, that had nothing to do with me. Why do you think I wanted to leave? You're the asshole that had to stay, solve the mystery. You want to blame someone, blame yourself."

Katy's voice was high, a slight whistle to her breathing. "Please tell me what the hell's going on. Are you guys doing this stuff on purpose? Is it . . . is it all fake?" Tears gathered in the corners of her eyes and Nate felt like shit. Aury had been right to keep Katy out of it. She needed it to be real.

"There is something there," said Aury, leaning in close. "It's not fake—that place is fucked up." She stared out the window. "That doesn't mean we should believe everything we see and hear while we're there. We've all watched ghost hunting shows—it's easy to get caught up in the moment, the atmosphere, and think we're seeing things that aren't there. And we can't discount the possibility of someone else interfering."

"You mean Stella?" he asked, surprised he hadn't thought of that before.

"Her, or one of the guys. Helter and Gunther."

Katy frowned. "I don't think they'd do something like that. Not Gunther."

"Either way, we should operate on the assumption it's real, to be safe, but we're likely to find natural explanations for at least some of it." Aury's even tone had its affect—Katy was calmer now, her breath returned to normal without need of her inhaler.

"Yeah, like those fucking fingers," Nate said, numb by now to the shock of those digits plunking down the stairs, the way the index finger curled in and back out again, beckoning him up that last flight of stairs. Had Aury been responsible for those, too? But how? Who could have thrown them, since everyone was accounted for? "What the fuck."

"Fuh . . . fingers?" stuttered Katy, her face going pale. Aury looked at him sharply.

Nate sat forward. "The fingers that fell down the stairs, right after that fucking noise stopped. You saw them, didn't you?"

Panic gripped his heart when neither said anything, Aury frowning, Katy's mouth open, eyes wide.

"Oh come the fuck on, we all saw them, they were *right* there—two fucking fingers with red painted nails."

Aury raised an eyebrow. "Was that what it was? The shit that came bouncing down from the top floor?"

"Yeah. They were fucking disgusting. You're telling me no one else saw them?"

She shrugged. "Maybe no one else was close enough, and then Stella stole the show with her little trip, so. That explains it."

But had Stella tripped? Was it really an accident? The optical illusion of the figure that stood in the shadows crowded into his head. Even in memory, Nate couldn't tell if it was there. Visible from one angle, but stare long enough and it resolves into something else. Looking at his sisters' faces, he knew better than to mention what he probably hadn't seen, anyway. They were having a hard enough time accepting the fingers.

Aury's voice softened. "We're not saying it didn't happen."

But no one was saying it did, either. Nate felt that same familiar pull of quicksand beneath his feet, the truth he knew sinking out of sight, obscured and ignored.

"No. Fuck this. I'm not crazy, and I'll prove it." He climbed out of the vehicle, slammed the door behind him. Head down, he pulled his phone from his pocket and turned his back on the bright lights of the hospital parking lot. It was still early, barely past four in the afternoon, but they were in the darkening season of short days and early dusk. He punched Carrie's name on his recent calls before he could think better of it.

She answered on the second ring. "Nate. How are you? Is Stella okay?"

He ignored her questions. "Can you come get me? I don't have my car. I'm still at the hospital." He paused, took a breath. "I need to go back."

Two beats of silence followed his words, then: "I'll be there in ten."

He hung up, already feeling better, then nearly screamed when a hand fell on his shoulder. He turned to find Aury on one side of him, with Helter of all people on the other.

"We're coming, too."

# CHAPTER THIRTEEN

**"WHO'S STAYING WITH STELLA?"** Nate asked as the four of them stood outside the house once more, full dark hiding the details in shadow, making it more menacing, less real.

"Do you care?" asked Carrie, her expression as tranquil as ever.

He shrugged. "No, actually."

"Okay, then." His mentor started up the walk, hands in her coat pockets. She wore jeans with holes in them and running shoes, at odds with the elegance of her wool jacket and leather messenger bag. She didn't look back to see if they'd follow, only stopping to wait for them once she reached the dark front stoop. "Key?"

Nate frowned. "We came outta here so fast before, I don't think anyone took the time to lock up. Should be open."

Carrie tried the handle but it wouldn't budge.

Helter cast a nervous glance at Aury before hurrying up behind her, brandishing the key. "I, uh, I went back and locked it, before I met you guys in the ER. All our gear's in there." He opened the place up, held the door for Carrie as she walked in without hesitation.

Aury leaned in. "I like her," she observed as they fell into step.

An involuntary smile pulled up one corner of Nate's mouth. "Yeah."

They followed Carrie's lead, the pale light of the half moon failing to penetrate past the first two steps inside.

"Lights?" asked Carrie.

"Um, I think we left all that stuff up there."

Nate looked up the stairs, suddenly regretting his rash decision to come here now, in the dark. He cast an uneasy glance around the shadowed rooms, looking for something hidden in the corners, motionless. Waiting. He pulled his gaze away with effort, held his breath and listened. Trying not only to hear, but to feel. Katy said before the atmosphere felt heavy. And then the shit happened with the noise, and the figure at the top of the stairs . . . was it the same one he thought he'd seen in Katy's closet? The one standing over Stella's crumpled body?

He didn't want to believe in any of this, tried to stick to the comfortable assumption Aury had done it all, but the things that scared him were harder to dismiss when he was inside the place. He knew what happened back then, and none of it was supernatural, just a banal, human monster. But now? He didn't know if they'd find those fingers when they got up there, but it was getting harder to deny there was *some* kind of presence here. Whatever he believed or didn't about the sound and the dreams, something called him up those stairs, made it almost a compulsion. And as much as he hated to agree with Stella about anything, it was hard to imagine who it could be, if not Shawn.

Carrie turned. "Well? Are we going up?"

Helter swallowed audibly, adjusted the camera on his shoulder. "Is it . . . do you guys think it's safe?"

Carrie cocked her head. "Yes, of course it's safe. Unless there's something up there you haven't told us about."

Helter dropped his gaze to the floor. "No. Just the usual stuff."

Carrie watched the kid in silence for a beat or two until Nate sidled closer to her, breathed in the clean, coconut scent of her shampoo. Immediately wanted to punch himself for the thought.

"You don't feel anything?" he asked in a low voice.

Aury frowned. She wouldn't know about Carrie.

Very few people did outside of select circles, especially since she conducted her other practice under a pseudonym.

Carrie shrugged, releasing Helter from her gaze. "I didn't say that. There's . . . " She frowned, looked up the dark staircase. "I don't know. There's darkness here, and a lot of other residual stuff, but it's hard to tell if it's anything over and above what you'd expect in any place this old. There doesn't seem to be anything malevolent. At least not as far as I can tell."

"Do you want to know the history before you go up?" asked Helter. "The stuff people have seen, since Stella left?"

Carrie fixed him with her gaze once more. "No. Shall we?"

Helter jogged to stay close to her, his mouth agog even as he kept the camera trained on her classic profile. Nate quashed a stab of jealousy as he and Aury followed at a more sedate pace, both of them casting nervous glances every step or so.

"So who is she, exactly?" asked Aury. "Not just your boss, it seems."

Nate shot a look up the stairs. "What? Of course she is. She's the most ethical person I know. There's nothing unprofessional about our relationship, so don't go reading shit into it."

Aury chuckled. "I meant her profession. Your standard psychiatrist doesn't usually moonlight as a human ghost meter, do they? So what's her deal?"

Blood rushed to Nate's face, embarrassment like a heat wave through his whole body. "Oh. No, she's not standard, not even close. Primarily what she does is the same thing I do, only a lot better. But she has this other part of her practice . . . "

"Clearly. That why you brought her?"

"Yes. Can we catch up to the others? I'm a grown man, but if that fucking noise starts up you're gonna hear me scream like an eight-year-old girl."

"Funny. I used to say when I was eight that you screamed like a scared forty-year-old man."

He snorted. "So, are you gonna tell me, now Katy's not here?"

"Tell you what?" she asked.

"You know what I mean. You've been dropping hints this whole time—you're up to something. I get why you want to keep Katy out of it, but this is me. So tell me now—how much of this is you?"

Her eyes finally met his. "You'll manufacture anything to avoid the truth, won't you?"

Her words stung, but he tried not to show it. "That's not an answer."

Aury raised her brows. "All I told you was this wasn't about Stella. That I had plans in place, because I'm not going to let her get control again—especially not here." She lowered her voice and drew closer. "So, yes. I funded this thing. I'm the one who found these guys, approached them about doing an episode on the fucked-up Lascos. I paid for the nice stuff upstairs, and a good chunk of that shiny new equipment Helter's dragging around, but that doesn't mean it's not real. I chose them specifically *because* they don't use special effects. They're low budget as hell, but I watched their earlier episodes—they *believe*." Her eyes were unreadable in the dim lighting. "That's what I wanted back then—someone to believe. And that's what we need now. I didn't create whatever lives here. I know you won't believe, no matter what the hell you experience, but trust me when I say this house doesn't need any help with atmosphere." She pulled her shoulders in, made herself smaller as she looked at the high ceilings, arching into blackness above. There could be anything up there waiting for them—anything at all.

Aury started climbing again and Nate hurried to catch up. "Aury, come on. I'm not trying to denigrate your experiences, but you can't expect me to believe—"

She halted and looked down at him, her lips tight, jaw

jutted. "I don't. I've never expected anything out of you—why would I start now?"

Nate's jaw dropped, flinching like she'd landed a fist in his gut. Before he could gather himself to respond, Carrie leaned over the second-floor landing and lifted an eyebrow.

"Found your fingers, Nate."

# CHAPTER FOURTEEN

**NATE STARED IN** fascinated disgust at the digits resting on the third stair, right where he'd left them in his haste to see if Stella truly was dead. It was a relief seeing them there, a balm to his panicked sense of unreality, the fear that no one would believe what he'd said. It was also terrifying.

"So they're . . . real? I mean, not plastic or something?" asked Helter, camera shaky but aimed at the fingers.

Nate's hopes rose—if the fingers were fakes, that propped up his theory that someone corporeal, whether Aury or not, was behind every weird-ass thing they'd seen.

Aury nudged one with her knuckle and grimaced. "Feel real."

"They smell real, too," commented Carrie.

Nate's nostrils flared and for the first time he caught the coppery tinge of blood, the slightly sweet smell of early rot. There was no way Aury did this. She believed in ghosts, not dismemberment. Disappointment dipped his stomach, and he frowned at the fingers. "Where's the blood? I mean, if these are fresh, wouldn't they at least be oozing or something?"

Carrie shrugged. "Who says they're fresh? How long ago did all this happen? Twenty years, right?"

"Well, yeah, but we're not seriously suggesting those are *Stella's*, are we? I mean, they can't be. Where would they have been all this time? Because whatever else I'm willing to believe, I'm not buying some ghost or whatever has been keeping them on ice for two decades." He resolutely shoved away the image of that index finger curling and uncurling on the stair. The damn thing wasn't sentient—it must have hit just right, been jolted by the fall.

"Hmm." Carrie dropped to one knee, nudging the siblings out of her way, and pressed her own fingertips to the severed flesh. Nate fought his gag reflex, wondering how everyone kept casually touching the severed fingers. "Maybe not ghosts, but these things have definitely been frozen. They've been thawing for a bit, but you can tell, the core of them is still really solid."

"Oh," said Helter, letting the camera drop from his shoulder. "I thought we really had something here." He looked at Aury. "Still, pretty creepy, right? And they got a reaction out of Stella."

Aury narrowed her eyes, lips pressed together as she considered the young man. "Maybe. I'm not entirely sure she saw them before taking her little swan dive. But maybe the reaction was the point."

Carrie pushed to her feet, wiping her hands on her holey jeans before retrieving a small bottle of hand sanitizer from her bag, passing it to Aury when she was done. "We still might have something, I'm just not sure what part this little perversity plays in it. They came from up there? Same as the sound?'

She started up the stairs even as she spoke, and Nate had to stop himself from grabbing her, pulling her back down. Whatever fear had fled in the face of the very real fingers flared again at the memory of that dark figure.

It was Aury who stopped her. "Wait. I'll buy that this shit is fishy—it's what I thought at the time, that it was too convenient. We'd barely started, but everything goes to hell as soon as we settle in on the second floor. Almost like it was on cue."

Both Lasco siblings looked at Helter and he turned red.

Carrie paused halfway up and turned back, resting a hand on the banister. Now the darkness loomed behind her and Nate's anxiety ratcheted further. At any second, whatever was up there could reach out, grab her and swallow her into the shadows. Or push her, sending her rolling end over end, and he didn't trust that she'd escape as unscathed as Stella. Only the good die young—evil fuckers hung on forever.

Her eyes were trained on Aury's. "What's your suspicion? You think someone did these things on purpose, planted them? The noise, and the fingers?"

Aury shrugged, her expression troubled, which sent Nate's fear skyrocketing. He still wanted to believe she was behind everything he'd seen, that she was pushing to extremes in the interests of undoing Stella. It was a convenient belief, but that didn't make it wrong.

"Maybe," Aury said. "I'd believe that easier than I do the idea that Shawn's just been dicking around here for twenty years, waiting to play pranks on us. If he *is* here, or if he shows up at some point, I don't see this being his grand entrance." She frowned. "And I'm no expert, but I've never seen a continuous *physical* manifestation of something like this. I don't think an entity would be capable."

It still made Nate uncomfortable, hearing his logical and reason-based sibling talk about the paranormal like it was a given, hauntings a common occurrence. It didn't fit with everything he knew about her, but then, how well did he know either of his sisters, beyond the roles Stella had cast them in?

"I tend to agree with that, given the information we have. So that leaves the question of who?" Carrie asked, casting a glance at Helter.

This time he had a response, though he still flushed bright red. "No way. Are you kidding? It totally fucked everything up—the whole point of this show was the reveal. That's what she promised us. We never expected to capture anything on camera, and these things showing up when they did—it doesn't further that goal."

Nate's eyes narrowed. "You never expected to capture anything? So what, your whole pitch was a lie? You don't think there's anything haunting this house?"

Helter swallowed hard, his face reddening as he backpedaled. "That's not what I meant. I believe in ghosts—Gunther and I both do, man. Believe me when I say we've seen some *shit*. But the human interest with you guys, with this place, is how it affected all of you. How whatever happened here is still haunting you, all this time later."

Nate thrust out his lower jaw, worked on keeping his temper in check. He didn't want to lose it in front of Carrie. He didn't want her to see the Nate his family knew, the one he tried to bury.

"Look, whether there's really something paranormal here or not, we want to *know*. We don't use special effects or anything like that. We're only interested in the real deal—that's what sets us apart."

Nate barked a short laugh and Helter glared. "Believe what you want, but we didn't have anything to do with the fucking fingers."

Carrie considered the kid, her intense study of his face stretching on for long, slow seconds while he fidgeted under her gaze. Finally she returned her attention to the Lascos. "Stella?"

Nate and Aury each raised a brow in unconscious imitation.

"It was pretty convenient," Nate said. "I knew from the start of this shitshow she wasn't going to tell us what happened."

Aury nodded slowly. "And if we believe it really was some ghost or demon or whatever, it supports her whole 'the ghosts made me do it' claim."

"But?" prodded Carrie, her gaze on Aury. "You were going to say something else a few minutes ago. The sound and the fingers, you think those were planted."

"Maybe, although fuck knows where she'd have found frozen fingers."

"Okay, so what was the other part?"

Aury looked at Nate. "You said you saw someone at the top of the stairs. Someone in shadow, and they're the one who kicked those things down the steps, right?"

Nate nodded warily, his cheeks burning where he felt Carrie watching him. "I mean I assume that's what happened. I didn't see the . . . figure, or whatever, move at all. But it's dark up there, so that doesn't mean much."

Aury shrugged. "We don't need to know the exact mechanics of it. But if all of us were accounted for, which we were . . . " She counted off names while pointing where each person was when Nate saw the figure on the stairs. "Me, Stella, Katy, Gunther, Helter, and Nate." She raised her eyes slowly to the top of the staircase. "Which means whoever might have planted that other stuff, someone else was here. Living or dead, we weren't alone here today. And chances are, we're not alone now."

# CHAPTER FIFTEEN

**A SWEEP OF** the house came up empty. No lurking presence, nothing to indicate there ever had been. The dark wooden floor at the top of the third story steps was covered in at least an inch of undisturbed dust, cobwebs hanging low from every corner, and Nate tried not to think about what that meant about the figure he'd seen at the top of the stairs. The windows up here were intact for the most part, too high up for vandals to easily hit. After a check of the immediate vicinity, they trudged down to the basement to start from the ground up, sticking together. There would be no splitting up under Carrie's watch.

With the electricity still turned off, the whole house was dark as hell, the basement as dim and unknowable as he'd expected. It was more of a generic creepiness, and Nate's apprehension grew once they reached the first floor—where the family had lived, spent time together. Made memories, mostly bad ones, and they waited around every corner. In the kitchen, the image of Stella's shadow preceding her, slinking over the tiled floor, moving as though independent of its maker. The walk-in pantry where Stella had once shoved Katy, slamming the door and locking it behind her, laughing hysterically the whole time. Nate remembered the bewildered look on Katy's tear-stained face when Shawn let her out—their mother either didn't know or didn't care how far she eroded her children's trust with each careless cruelty. The living room where the three youngest would argue over the television, not noticing the retreat of the oldest Lasco sibling. Nate wondered when Shawn had first withdrawn from the family, and why the hell none of them thought about it, understood the significance. Tears burned the back of his eyes with each half-buried recollection. They had failed Shawn, all of them.

With each door they entered, Nate expected to see the shadow form lurking. Several times he thought he did, but it was a trick of the light, resolving itself to nothing once he'd blinked a few times. Gradually the place grew less creepy as they'd combed over it together, methodically clearing every room in turn. Nate knew how much that had to do with Carrie being there. She was unemotional and matter of fact, and in her calm presence many of the shadows of childhood fled. Even when they checked Katy's old room together, she parted the closet doors without hesitation, and nothing jumped out at them, or lurked in a dark corner.

His fear returned once they mounted the steps to the third floor again. His palms were slick with sweat and he couldn't seem to catch his breath, resolutely shoving away the feeling of slow suffocation. Psychosomatic, a result of his dreams.

The four of them stopped in front of the third-floor door, standing in the center of an otherwise open plan layout. It was more like a loft up here, set deep across the back half of the house, the main room open to a balcony-style overlook. It struck him how odd the placement of the door was, the room as a whole. Smack in the middle of things, like a portal to somewhere else. If he remembered correctly, the walls had been soundproofed, too, and he squirmed thinking of all the reasons someone would have done that to a random room at the top of the house. The place had bad energy; even he could feel that. He stood unmoving, his eyes locked on the door that changed everything.

Aury had been right—remnants of what he assumed

was crime scene tape fluttered in spots, the adhesive long worn away. It was enough to confirm the door hadn't been opened since that night, or whenever the police had released the scene. Nate shivered. Even if Helter and Gunther had trumped up the haunted history, people lived here after Stella left for good. Why the hell wouldn't someone, *anyone* have opened it?

Aury moved to stand beside him, Carrie just in front. Helter came up breathlessly, the heavy camera dragging at his left arm, tucking his phone back in his pocket with his right.

"Gunther just called. They're all good. Stella's awake, doc says she's fine, no injuries but for some contusions. She got really lucky."

Aury and Nate exchanged another wordless look. Lucky was one word for it.

"And Katy? How's she?" asked Nate, his attention drawn inexorably back to the door. The wood was darker than he remembered, with what looked like stains in strange patterns. It was too easy to picture blood spatter soaking in and making those shapes, but the carnage had been on the other side. Surely the wood was too thick for anything to bleed through?

"She's okay. Still pretty shaky, and definitely not up for coming out here, but Gunther's staying with her for now. He'll drop her off at her fiancé's place when she's ready."

Nate nodded and blew out a breath. "Okay. So we gonna do this?"

Helter frowned. "Open it, you mean? Don't we need everyone else here? And we're not even filming with our good gear. This is gonna look like amateur hour."

His protests petered out under Carrie's steady gaze. Then she turned to the brother and sister.

"He has a point. Not about the filming, but the inclusion aspect. Doesn't Katy deserve to be here for this?"

Nate took a step closer. "No way, you heard him. She's not up for coming back here, and I don't blame her. So we'll do it for her—get a look and give her the CliffsNotes version, then she can make up her mind about whether she wants to come back and see it for herself."

Carrie studied him. "You make it sound like the answer you want from Stella is on the other side of that door. Do you believe that?"

Nate flushed under her gaze. "No," he muttered. "I guess not. It's just . . . this is what I came here for. This is why I agreed to do this fucking stupid show in the first place. I wanted to know. And maybe . . . " He looked at Aury. "We never saw it, after what happened. Our imaginations filled in the gaps, but if we could just look at it . . . maybe we could understand what went down."

It sounded dumb when he said it out loud. He knew damn well whatever evidence there was, whatever the crime scene consisted of, would have been cleared long ago.

"Do we even have the key?" asked Aury.

Nate frowned. "The key? You're telling me it's locked? I thought it was just taped."

She shook her head. "It was locked when I lived here. You don't think I tried?"

He lifted a shoulder. "You said, about the tape . . . you made it sound like it was a respect issue or something."

"And did I strike you as a respectful teenager? Come on, any of us would have tried. But when I did, it was locked. I must have tried to pick it a hundred times, but I couldn't do it. I even broke down and asked Stella for the key—she wouldn't tell me where it was."

Everyone turned to Helter, who shrugged. "Not it, guys."

Nate glared. "What the fuck—how were you planning on getting in there, then? This was your reveal and you didn't have a way in?"

"Your mom said she had it. Wanted to hang onto it. I couldn't convince her otherwise, so I didn't have much choice but to go along with it."

"Stella has it? Fuck!" screamed Nate, throwing his hands in the air, dropping his head back and letting his anger flow. Helter flinched, took two steps away from him, but neither Aury nor Carrie reacted. Nate stomped over to the door and seized the knob, gave it a vicious twist, but it stuck tight, not budging an inch.

"Fuck, fuck, fuck!" he screamed again, knowing his anger was all out of proportion to the circumstances and not caring. He threw his shoulder into the wood, dust flying into his face, translucent shreds of tape floating in his peripheral vision. The door remained as solid and impassive as it had twenty years ago. His sixteen-year-old fury and desperation hadn't moved it back then, and it didn't do so now. After thirty or so seconds of fruitless assault, he let his forehead drop and hit the wood with a thud, shame flooding in to take the place of his anger. "Goddamn it," he muttered, giving the door one last half-hearted thump.

His outburst having silenced everyone else, the responsive *thump* from inside the room echoed through the house.

"Fuck," hissed Aury, grabbing Nate's arm to pull him back.

"What the hell was that?" asked Helter, his voice shaking.

Carrie cast a glance at him. "That camera running? Let's make sure to get the audio."

He nodded, and she stepped forward, gave the door a sharp knock. They all held their breaths, but the house remained silent.

"Okay, so maybe I knocked something off a shelf, or leaning up against a wall," whispered Nate.

Carrie studied him. "Try it again."

Aury pulled at his arm again, glared at the other woman. "Are you fucking nuts? No, don't go back over there."

He tried to smile. "I don't believe in this shit, remember?"

"And since when was that a requirement for danger? You think you're dealing with faeries that need you to clap for them to exist? It doesn't work like that." When he tried to pull away she held tighter, made him meet her eyes. "Remember, Nate—alive or dead, someone was at the top of these stairs. And someone is behind that door."

Nate turned to Helter, who was no use, pointing the camera everywhere like he thought it was a weapon, exhilaration trying to overtake his fear.

Finally Nate raised a brow at Carrie, who shrugged.

"I can't tell," she said in answer to his unasked question.

"Can't tell *what*?" asked Aury. "You got X-ray vision or something?"

Nate patted the hand she'd wrapped around his bicep and pulled gently away. This time she let him go. "This is why we're here, remember?"

"No, it's not," she muttered, but made no move to restrain him again.

Nate did it in a rush, not giving himself time to chicken out. He gave three knocks, hard enough to make his knuckles sting, sparking a sickly tremor of memory.

*Thump, thump, thump* came the sound from the other side.

Aury did scream this time, and it turned his heart cold. Aury was never afraid. She was never *anything,* at least not before they'd come back to this place. But something was on the other side of that door, and Nate couldn't leave without knowing what, or who, it was. His throat dry, heartbeat loud in his ears, he gently laid his cheek against the smooth wood, the fingertips of both hands splayed lightly on the surface. He closed his eyes and pictured something doing the same on the other side, pressing a rotted cheek only inches away from his own. Staring through the wood with nothing eyes.

"What the *fuck*, Helter?" his sister asked.

"I fucking swear to God, it's not me—we didn't have the

key! We didn't set this up—there's something in there, and it's got nothing to do with the damn show."

Tears spilling from her cold blue eyes, Aury grabbed Nate again and pulled. "We're going. Now."

Nate was about to protest, demand they get something to break the door down when all at once Shawn's scent washed over him, just as Katy and Aury had described. It was more than his body wash: warmer, tinged with the undercurrents of sweat and stale cigarettes that brought his brother back to him, and a crippling grief filled him. It swept in a physical arc of pain through his back, shoulders and legs, buckling his knees.

A cool hand on his neck made the pain ebb, eased it back enough that he could breathe through the weight of it. Carrie stood at his side, her own scent covering that of his brother, and even in his relief he wanted to scream at her to back off, not to take this from him.

"What do you want to do?" she asked.

Before he could answer, the house juddered, the floor vibrating against his feet as that terrible grinding sound began. This time there was no build up, no soft entrance as warning, just that deep bass scrape over and over, reverberating through his teeth and spine. Worse than that, it seemed to stir something within his gut, a sickening, heavy feeling as though the other Nate who'd crawled inside him was waking, summoned by the sound.

Shawn's scent and imagined proximity fled as Nate's courage crumbled. His desire to know was eclipsed by a desperate need to get away from the noise, to quiet the beast inside him. It was a graceless dash down both flights of stairs, Aury's hand in his, following close on Helter's heels as they ran. The noise didn't stop until they spilled into the frigid night air, and in the sudden silence Nate's ears rang, his jaw aching from that heavy, rhythmic grinding. Now, outside the house, the silence and apparent peace of the place weighed heavier than everything else. This was how it always looked to outsiders. Dark and quiet, nothing wrong at all. No hint of the shadows within, the constant turmoil and emotional pain.

Except . . . there *was* a shadow, up there in the third-floor window. Or not a shadow, exactly, because it was instead a smudge of lighter color standing out against the darkness within. Nate squinted, waiting for it to resolve itself into something innocuous, a reflection of moonlight in the glass perhaps, but instead the pale blur raised a hand and pressed it to the glass.

Nate choked on a cry, stumbled back.

"Nate? Are you okay?" Carrie's brows were drawn, mouth turned down. Her worried look. She was the last one out of the house, moving with measured steps, closing the door behind her as she tucked something in her coat pocket.

Nate looked up at the window again, but whatever had been there was gone. "Fine," he lied, wiping a hand over his mouth. Telling himself he didn't feel the yawning pit of grief opening in his gut. Insisting his cowardice hadn't cost him his chance to see his brother once more.

Carrie pursed her lips but nodded, continuing down the stairs until she stopped in front of the siblings. "Any idea what that sound was?"

Aury's gaze dropped and she wiped her eyes. Nate shrugged, his hands shaking hard. He couldn't stop himself from staring at that window. "It's the same thing we heard before, and I'm no closer to placing it."

She nodded and turned back to the house. "So what's next? Does the show go on?"

"No," said Nate flatly, turning his back. "Not like this. We're not getting anywhere, and it's not . . . look, whatever's going on in there, it's not healthy for any of us to be here." He glared at Helter. "I thought this was going to be a one-day deal, that we'd get our answers or we wouldn't, but either way it'd be over. I didn't sign up for a fucking mini-series. Was the reveal even going to happen today?"

The younger man shrugged uncomfortably. "That was the plan originally, but Stella said . . . she wanted more time. Needed a chance to work up the courage to go in there. I didn't like it, but without her, there's no show."

"There isn't one, anyway." Nate turned on his heel, shoved his frozen hands into his pockets.

Helter chased after him. "Nate, seriously, you gotta have some faith. You're going to get what you want—we've made huge progress, can't you see that? That house is *humming*. We're so fucking close—you can't walk away now."

Nate was deaf to Helter's protests, but his sister grabbed his arm once more. When he turned to face her, the mask of ice was back in place, colder than ever.

"I came here for a reason. I know you did, too." Her gaze flicked to the pocket where Shawn's knife lay and Nate flushed in the darkness.

"I'm not leaving without answers. Without making her feel what we felt." Her grip was hard enough to make him wince, her fingers digging deep into the muscle of his arm.

"What exactly is Stella claiming, with respect to the supernatural?" asked Carrie, still studying the house.

Nate shrugged. "Not sure. It's not a coherent narrative, something about shadows and heaviness. She's hinted about something else, something from before we moved in, but she hasn't said what. The ghosts made her do it, that's all I gathered."

Carrie frowned. "From *before* you moved in? Like what?"

Aury shrugged. "She hasn't gone into detail. I've looked into the history of the place and didn't find anything. No murders, not even any deaths I can find reference to, and no one reported any disturbances until after we lived here. Property manager thought that was probably power of suggestion, anyway, once people knew about Shawn's death."

"Hm. And what do you think? You lived here the longest. Any truth to it?"

Aury frowned, releasing her hold on Nate. "Like I said, I didn't find anything to corroborate it in the property records. But a while back she started asking me questions about what I remembered from the house. Did I have any strange experiences there, feelings that didn't seem like my own. See anyone that didn't belong."

"Did you?" asked Carrie, her expression blank.

Aury took a deep breath, looked back up at the house. "I did. We all did, even if some of us repressed it."

Nate pursed his lips. "Oh come the fuck on, Aury, don't buy into this shit. When you talked me into this, you said, you told me it was a fucking ruse, a way to get her to confess. Now you're going along with it?"

Aury's face was stony. "I don't think I called it a ruse. I said it could work regardless of what anyone else believed, as long as we catered to Stella's version of reality." She looked at the frozen ground, her voice lowering. "It's not just her. I told you before, I experienced things. And not just after you two left—we *all* felt *something*. You don't remember hiding under that gross old blanket in the den, trying not to breathe so it wouldn't find us?"

He opened his mouth to deny it, to call it out for the fiction it was. But a sense memory overwhelmed him. The sour smell of the unwashed blanket, covered in pet hair from animals long dead. The scratchy feel of ancient goose feathers poking from the dingy cloth covering. The chest tightening feeling of running out of fresh air under there, the increasing need to throw it back and gasp in oxygen. And the limb freezing terror of revealing himself to something that cast its shadow over where all four of them hid. He closed his mouth and kept quiet.

Carrie spoke as if the exchange hadn't happened. She was trained not to take notice of these little family outbursts, after all, and Nate felt a spreading shame at being part of one. "And these questions of Stella's—they just came out of nowhere? Had she claimed supernatural agency before this?"

"No," said Nate, but Aury pursed her lips. "Not to me," he amended.

Carrie nodded. "But she did to you?" she asked Aury.

"Yes. Not immediately, I don't think. We didn't talk about much of anything the first couple months after . . . well, after."

"But then?" Carrie prompted.

"Yes. She brought it up one night while we were watching television on the couch. Just started talking about it like it was a conversation she was picking back up. Chatting about the ghost who haunted her the whole time, like I was supposed to know." She gave a brittle laugh. "She told me I did—insisted we'd discussed it before, that all of us knew about it."

Nate took a breath, remembering Stella's proficiency at recreating history. Denying the experiences of her children in favor of a more pleasant truth. He supposed to a mother who could murder her son, a killer ghost probably looked like a good alternative.

"Then after the house was sold, and we moved out, she never talked about it again. Acted like it never happened, like I imagined the whole thing."

Carrie cocked her head. "So what changed? What brought her back around to all this?

"You remember her saying Shawn visited her at night?" Aury asked.

Nate had thought his rage was spent, that he had no fuel left for the fire, but he was wrong. His face burned and he ground his teeth. "She's full of shit."

Aury's face was unreadable.

"What, you're not gonna tell me you believe that crap? Even if I buy the idea of the paranormal, I sure as shit don't believe Shawn's been hanging out on the end of her bed, reviving that loving mother-son relationship." His words dripped venom, but he didn't give two craps.

"My point is, it doesn't actually matter if she's lying, or delusional, or telling the truth. Seeing him was the impetus for her doing this whole circus, and I plan to see it through."

Carrie turned her attention to Helter. "What did she tell you, when you first talked to her about the show?"

Helter shuffled his feet, looked at Aury, then dropped his gaze. "She said she wanted to clear her name. That there was something dark in this house, and that was why her son was dead."

Nate scrubbed a hand over his face, exhaustion flooding through his body as the adrenaline leached away. "Great. More fucking lies. Why the hell did I agree to this shit?"

"For Katy," Aury said softly.

His shoulders sagged, then he lifted his chin and looked at Carrie, gaze narrowed. "She's claiming possession, right? Is that what we're getting from all this?"

Carrie frowned at him. "No, Nate. We're not doing that."

He shook his head, energy buzzing through him again. "Not a real one, but to make a point. The only way we're going to win this game, get what we want, is to play along with her." He looked at Aury. "Like we always used to have to. Like you've still been doing—same as the bullshit with her getting my name wrong. Easier to ride the crazy train than convince it to jump the track."

She nodded slowly, frowning. "So you want to like, have an exorcism or something? I don't think that's going to do much but give her a chance to spit pea soup at us and cuss in new languages."

Carrie's focus stayed on Nate. "It doesn't work like that, and you know it," she said, displeasure evident in her voice. It wasn't secret, what she did, but it also wasn't a game. "Besides, you don't believe in possession."

"No, I don't," he said with unwonted emphasis. "And I'm not asking for an exorcism, because you're right, that won't work. But a séance, or something along those lines. A cleaning, if you will," he said with a grin at Helter. "You guys say you clean houses, right? And if it really was something other than Stella, something evil that was responsible for Shawn's death, or if she wants to convince us it was, then she'll have to agree to a ritual to expel it, right?"

Aury nodded slowly, lips pursed, thinking it over. "And if it's the 'ghost' or whatever confessing, then she can get all those gory details out, the things she wants to make sure we know, and it won't even be her talking. I don't care if she blames it on a ghost, as long as she says the words. See how well that shit holds up in court, anyway."

Nate nodded, smiling. "And she can't say no, because that'll mean she's either admitting it's bullshit, or that she doesn't want to be free of it."

He turned to Carrie, gripped his hands together. "Please. I know it's not how or why you usually do things like this. But I can feel it—this is the way forward. For all of us."

Aury frowned. "I don't get it. I thought this was your boss, so she's a counselor too, right?"

"A psychiatrist," Nate corrected. "And I told you before, she has a separate practice for other services. She knows all about this kind of shit."

"What, ghost shit?"

Everyone was looking at Carrie now, and she gave them a slight smile and sighed. "Family shit. Emotional shit, and the blowback it causes. Most so-called hauntings are actually just a build-up of strong, residual emotion. Sometimes people need help clearing it out, so they can move on."

Aury's jaw dropped. "And you . . . you *do* that?"

"Why, yes, I do. Rather well, actually. If you think about it, spiritual cleansing is a natural outgrowth of therapy."

Helter looked at her with new respect, eyes wide. "So we get to do a fucking *séance?* Wicked!"

Nate bit his lip, searching for the words to convince

her, but before he could speak again she lifted her chin and nodded.

"You'll do it?" he asked.

She shrugged. "You're right, this is exactly what I do. Help families in turmoil to clear out the bad shit. It's unorthodox, certainly, but if ever a family needed a cleanse . . . " She looked back up at the house, gaze lingering on the empty third-floor window. "And there *is* something dark here. Very dark. If we do it right, we can kill two birds with one stone."

Aury's lips curled in a smile. "Now *that's* what we're here for."

# CHAPTER SIXTEEN

**IT WAS EMBARRASSINGLY** easy to get Katy's cooperation, and Nate felt like dirt for deceiving her. Was he any better than Stella?

"Of course," she said, and even over the phone he could tell her whole face had lit up. "That's brilliant—it's exactly the kind of help Mom needs. And then she'll see that we believe her, that we're on her side, not plotting against her."

Nausea took an uneasy swim through Nate's stomach. Guilt always manifested in his gut, resulting in endless ulcers and digestive issues, to the point that food was more of a minefield than a pleasure. The thought brought a wave of relief with it—that ridiculous stirring in his belly, what else would it have been but his usual stomach upsets? He was an idiot to let those dreams get to him so badly. "Right, exactly."

"Oh, Nate, you can't imagine how happy this makes me. I'm literally dancing right now—she's going to be *thrilled*. Can I be the one to tell her? Please?"

Nate swallowed back a splash of stomach acid. "Of course." He'd been planning to ask her anyway, knowing if it came from him Stella would suspect a hidden agenda.

"Can you imagine if it *works*? I mean, this is your boss, I'm sure she's amazing so *of course* it'll work—it's just hard to wrap my head around the idea that this nightmare might finally be over. We might get our mom back, and I . . . " Her voice became suspended with tears and she soon ended the call, but not before thanking him. "You're wonderful, Nate. Truly the best big brother ever."

Nate put his head in his hands and dropped to his couch, considering heading out the door and straight into traffic. Best big brother, shit. Shawn would have been. He'd have held them together, brought them through even if they did irritate the piss out of him.

Nate thought about what his brother would look like now, if he'd lived. What kind of man he'd be, if Stella had given him the chance. He'd have been a good guy, the kind of solid dude his friends and family could rely on. Shawn wouldn't have believed that—Stella had him so twisted back then, he'd bought into the persona she'd created for him. Subject to ungovernable rage. Violent, dangerous. Damaged. None of that shit was true, and he'd have seen that once he got away from home. There'd be some screw ups in college, if he'd ended up going, but by now, he'd be on the right path. He was the one who always did the right thing, no matter how scary it was. If he were here now, everyone would be better off. Instead all they had was Nate, less than a shadow in comparison, and what kind of trade was he? Manipulating his little sister, using his intimate knowledge of her weaknesses to push her where he wanted her. His mother's son, after all.

And if he held up a mirror right now, who would be looking out from his eyes?

He dropped four ice cubes into a high ball and filled it to the rim, staring at the amber liquid as he held it close to his face before drowning his sorrows the best way he knew how.

\*\*\*

"She said no."

Nate groaned and clutched at the sides of his head, cradled in a way he hoped would stop the incessant, miserable pounding. "Why?" he finally managed, keeping his eyes shut tight even behind his sunglasses. Anger made the hangover worse, sending his blood pumping too fast through aching, inflamed veins, but he no longer had defenses against his fury. Everything he'd built, every excruciating inch he'd gained getting away from Stella, it had all crumbled beneath her first assault.

*Which is perfectly normal and not a fucking sign you were actually possessed in a dream, idiot.*

He groaned, clutching his belly. A deafening *clunk* sounded as a metal trash can was deposited in front of him, and he gave in to the demands of his stomach with relief. Once he'd voided his gut he wiped his mouth, sucking in air in the brief moments he had before the nausea returned. Aury handed him a cold water bottle and he drank it down, telling himself it was all he needed to set him straight.

"Where the hell'd you get this?" he asked, nudging the can away with his foot.

"I took it from behind the reception desk."

"And they didn't say anything?"

She shrugged. "Maybe. I wasn't listening. They got a problem with it, they can add it to the bill."

He coughed and spat. "Miss Moneybags over here. Does Stella even have insurance?" He didn't know if she had a job, let alone benefits, but there hadn't been any problems getting her admitted.

Aury shrugged, looked away.

"Seriously? You're not paying this shit out of pocket, are you?"

She gave him a tight smile. "Who do you think's been paying her bills up til now?"

He frowned, opened his mouth to protest but she mowed over him.

"You smell like a fucking distillery, you know."

Her words triggered his gag reflex and he bent over the trashcan once more, his sister silent at his side, a cool hand on the back of his neck.

"Did Stella say why she won't do it?" he asked again,

when the throbbing in his head eased enough for him to speak.

"Because of your girl. Doesn't like her."

Nate pinched the bridge of his nose beneath the sunglasses. "My girl?"

"Carrie. Little Ms. Ouija Board."

He cast a careful glance in her direction. Sudden movements were very bad for his health. "The fuck is that supposed to mean? They've never even met."

Aury laughed, but softly, and it occurred to him that for someone who didn't drink, she was awfully empathetic to hangovers.

"Has logic or experience ever gotten in the way of Stella's worldview? I assume she looked her up."

He frowned. "Even so. Carrie keeps her online footprint pretty bare bones. Why would Stella have a problem with her?"

"Why do you think? I'm betting she was able to find a picture, and Carrie's younger, more attractive, more successful. Plus it takes attention away from her. Stella sees this whole thing like her sweet sixteen party, or a prom or something, with her as queen. She doesn't want anyone taking away from that, and you gotta admit, Carrie's pretty striking."

Nate sighed, drank more water. "I've spent most of my professional life trying *not* to admit that."

Aury laughed and patted his knee. "Look at you, big bro, human after all." She eyed him for a moment. "So you been hittin' that or what?"

He coughed out a mouthful of water. "Jesus, I feel like I'm in a locker room."

"That's not an answer."

He kept his gaze between his feet, hoping she'd move on, but she'd always been good at waiting. "No, I'm not *hitting* that."

"But you wanna be."

Nate felt a different flutter in his stomach and flushed. "Yeah, I guess I do, in the abstract."

"In the *abstract?* Wow, you even make sex sound clinical."

"All I mean is, yes, I'm attracted to her. But I also work with her, and I have no reason to believe she feels the same way." Saying it out loud was unexpectedly deflating, and he wrapped his arms around himself. "It's probably just transference, anyway. I'll get over it."

"Don't get over it too quick," she murmured, and he turned too fast to look at her, his head swimming at the sudden movement.

"Why? Do you think . . . I mean, did it seem like—"

She smiled. "Like you have a chance? Maybe. I don't know. It's not like I have a lot of experience with romance."

The wistful note in her voice took him by surprise. It must have shown on his face, as one brow rose and she turned the smile to a smirk. "You think I don't get crushes? Wish I was the kind of person who could act on them?"

He blinked, searching for the words to ease her sadness. She always managed to help him, always knew the right thing to say. But before his aching brain could come up with anything, she put her mask back on.

"Anyway. Hottie or not, Carrie's the reason Stella's set against the séance."

He debated steering her back to the subject of love lives, but he knew that face. She'd closed down, and if he pushed she'd retreat further. Besides, he still didn't know what to say—all the Lasco children were emotionally stunted, and he didn't have the tools to help his sister. All his training, his advanced degrees, and he couldn't help the people that mattered most. So he followed her lead and let it go. "So what the fuck do we do? How do we get her to agree?"

She shrugged, wrapped herself tighter against the cold. Nate hadn't wanted to enter the hospital, knowing how the smells of antiseptic would hit him, and she hadn't complained about sitting out here instead. She never did, and he suddenly felt guilty. How many times over the course of their lives had he taken advantage of that? He knew better than most that her silence didn't mean she wasn't hurting.

"I really don't want to go back in there," she said, sounding tired.

"The house? I thought you were gung-ho."

Aury grimaced. "The hospital. Had enough to last me a lifetime. Bad associations."

Nate nodded mechanically, then frowned. "When did you spend time in hospitals? For Stella?" It was entirely possible he'd missed a major injury or illness, Aury protecting her siblings from the knowledge. Saving Katy the worry and Nate the guilt that he didn't give a shit.

She shook her head, gaze still on the imposing building before them.

"For you?" he asked, dread gripping his gut. He couldn't take any more bad news—not right now.

She nodded slowly. "Yeah. Not the best experience. Do not recommend."

His mouth was dry. "What happened? Are you okay?"

She lifted a shoulder. "Seem to be. Been in remission almost a year now, and so far my scans look good."

Heat drained from his cheeks, his face going cold. "Remission. You . . . you have cancer?" He tripped over the word, alien and heavy. A bad luck word that conjured every superstition—don't let it hear you. Don't draw its notice, bring the curse down on those you love.

She noticed his stumble and smiled faintly. "Had cancer," she corrected. "Finished treatment a while ago."

He coughed, relief refusing to take hold. "What kind?"

"Ovarian."

Nate was at a loss for words. "But you're . . . you're not . . . "

"Gonna die?" she supplied.

Again the speaking of a superstition, a summoning of the reaper. He fought the urge to hush her, not push her luck. It was her life, and she'd earned the right to say it.

He cleared his throat. "Yeah."

"Some day. But not any time soon, and probably not from ovarian cancer. Fallopian tubes crossed."

It took his sluggish brain a second to catch up to her joke and he smiled. Hesitating for a moment, he reached out and laid a hand on her arm. "I'm glad you're okay."

"Thanks."

It bothered him she hadn't said anything at the time, but he got it. Keeping a brave face, not showing weakness of any kind—it was a learned trait. "You know if you're dealing with something like that . . . you can always tell me. I'll be there for you." He spoke awkwardly, avoiding her eyes.

"I'm telling you now."

"Thank you. For trusting me with it, I mean."

She patted his hand, then pulled away from his touch. "Anyway. Not to bring the mood down. We still need to get Stella on board with this séance."

Nate studied her profile, letting puzzle pieces click together in his muddled brain. The séance. Aury's previously undisclosed belief in ghosts and the afterlife. It made perfect sense—remission or not, cancer was still a wake-up call. She needed to believe in something, and he'd be damned if he'd be the one to take it away. He promised himself he'd be more open-minded, for her sake.

"So what do we do? Bribe her?"

Aury snorted. "More than I already have?"

His gaze narrowed. "I hate that she's been bleeding you dry all these years."

She shrugged. "It's just money. I don't need it all."

"I know, but—"

"She might listen to you," Aury interrupted.

Nate started to laugh but immediately regretted it, his headache ramping up again. "Me? She fucking hates me. I'm the one who ruined our family, remember? We hadn't spoken in years before yesterday, why would she listen to anything I say?"

Aury gave a dry laugh. "Because you have a dick, brother dear."

He snorted. Their mother had always been more prone to listen to members of the male sex—Aury or Katy could tell her something til they were blue in the face, but it took an endorsement from their uncle or one of their brothers before Stella would listen. Shawn thought it was hilarious, used it to his advantage more than once. Why couldn't Nate do the same thing?

*Because she doesn't see you as a real man. Because she knows you're the weak one, you always have been, and she'll find a way to exploit it.*

*Fuck it.*

Nate pushed off the bench and struggled to his feet. "Okay. Worth a fuckin' try." He looked down at the repulsive trash can. "What do I do with that?"

"My advice is to throw it in the nearest dumpster. You going in now?"

He blew out an unsteady breath and straightened his shoulders. "No time like the present. I have a dream of being done with all this shit by the time I get in bed tonight."

"Good. Me, too. Just don't mention I had anything to do with this plan. She'll do the opposite of whatever I suggest, so it's better she doesn't know this is something I want, too."

"Which just proves what a dumbass she is. You're the smartest out of all of us—always have been." He glanced down at her and suffered a shock when he saw her reddened nose, a single tear slipping beneath her shades. She hadn't even gotten misty-eyed talking about her cancer diagnosis.

"Oh, fuck off already," she said in a husky voice. "Don't go being nice, it ruins my mystique."

Stella was propped up on a bank of snow-white pillows, commanding the attention of at least two nurses and a young intern. Her manicured hands danced through the air like an orchestra conductor, punctuating an endless stream of commands, no less graceful for the loss of those two fingers. She looked fine, no indications of injury, glowing in fact, though that was likely a result of the attention.

As soon as she saw him at the door she put a hand to the back of her head, shrinking against the sheets. "Oh, my aching head. Isn't there anything you can do for it, Doctor?" she simpered, and Nate had to swallow back his disgust. He wondered how many layers of masks she wore, whether there'd be anyone at all underneath once she'd peeled the last one off. Had he ever even met the real Stella? Had anyone?

The intern promised to send someone in with painkillers and led the nurses out. Nate studied their faces for signs of annoyance, but there were none. Stella was excellent at making people like her, as long as she didn't have to keep it up for long.

"My darling son," she said, holding a quavering hand out to him, lips trembling, brow artfully furrowed. He had the overwhelming urge to high five her instead of the dramatic clasp she seemed to expect, overdo it so her hand smacked right back in her face. He compromised by keeping his hands in his pockets.

"Hey, Nate," said Katy in a low voice and he turned, surprised. He hadn't seen her tucked against the wall by the head of the bed. Her glow was gone, eyes dull, and she hadn't brushed her hair. He wondered if she'd had bad dreams again. Every ounce of her disappointment clung to her features—it hurt his heart and he took a deep breath. For Katy. And for Aury, even if she'd throw him out a window for suggesting it.

"Hey, kiddo," he said, giving her a smile before turning to their mother. "So I hear you're afraid of doing the séance?"

She pressed her lips into a thin line, pale eyes narrowing. "I didn't say anything about being afraid."

He raised his eyebrows. "Oh, I must have misunderstood."

"Who told you that—Aury? I swear, that girl's never happy unless she's spreading lies about me. It's sad, really, to see how jealous she is of her own mother. She can't *stand* not being the center of attention." She flipped her dark hair over one shoulder, crossing her arms.

Nate thought back on childhood memories in which his oldest sister featured only rarely. She'd always been the quiet one, stayed out of the way, mostly watching. Hell, she hadn't told any of them about her cancer—Stella would have taken out a billboard, if it were her. Aury was nothing like their mother. Center of attention was the last thing she wanted, but he did what Aury always did and let Stella keep her warped version of reality around her like a cocoon.

"If you're not afraid, what's the problem? I thought we were going to get rid of this thing. Don't you want your life back?"

"Of course I do, I'd do *anything* for my children, no matter how ungrateful, but I don't trust that Barker woman. She's nothing but a lying snake in the grass, and I won't have her interfering, twisting things to make me look bad. Besides, she's unprofessional, and probably a total fraud. And that hair color is *not* natural."

Nate clenched his fists but reminded himself Carrie wouldn't give a flip for what Stella said about her. "So you're familiar with her work? I didn't realize you knew her other name. How'd you find it?"

She shrugged, her eyes darting away, then back again. "I'm not an idiot. I can use the internet, you know."

Nate knew Carrie didn't publish a damn thing about her work with haunted families. It was word of mouth only, a hushed referral network. Stella was full of shit, making up accusations on the spot, but she'd never admit it. It didn't stop him needling her. "Which case do you think was fraudulent?"

She looked away from him and sniffed. "All of them. She's just in it for the money."

"Oh, does she charge a lot now? Weird, last I checked her rates it was the same as her hourly, which is pretty reasonable."

Stella glared at him. "Are you taking *that woman's* side against me?"

Nate lifted a shoulder. "I didn't think there were sides here. Carrie's my colleague, and she's great at what she does. I asked her for help because I know how good she is, and because I want the very best for you." He almost choked on his words, and hoped he didn't sound as insincere as he felt. "I guess we'll just cancel everything. I'll call Helter."

He turned but she clawed at his sleeve, tugged him back. He looked down at her, brows up. "What's the problem?"

"Don't you dare tell him that," she hissed between clenched teeth. "This isn't about you, or her, it's about *me*. I'm the one they want, I'm the reason for the whole show, so don't think you can take this from me." The sharp edges of her tone softened to a martyr's whine. "Of course I'll do the séance, I'll do whatever anyone asks of me. I always have, haven't I? But I want someone else. I don't trust that woman."

Nate shrugged. "We already discussed it with Helter and Gunther this morning. It's Carrie or no one—they've got a filming schedule to keep, and no time to track down someone else."

Katy cast a frowning glance at him and he kicked himself, hoping she wouldn't call him out on his lie. Of course she'd been in touch with Gunther—people naturally gave Katy the attention and care Stella demanded. The poor guy was probably half in love, and if he'd met her a few years ago, she might have already moved in with him.

Katy always used to move fast in love, finding the next great guy who made all the other ones look like dirt beneath their feet. Until they inevitably turned out to be the same kind of trash she'd been attracted to her whole life. Her own personal version of the Lasco legacy.

To his relief, she kept silent, so Nate was able to stand his ground with Stella. She stewed, threatened, shed tears, but he stood impassive. He played the role of Aury, letting his mother's threats and accusations roll over him, and he didn't even have to fake the faint smile on his face.

Finally, in a burst of tears, she gave in. "I'll do it for you kids," she said on a sob. "Even though I know she won't help. If it doesn't work, which it won't, then that's on her, not me. Never let it be said I didn't do everything I could."

He smiled to mask his disgust, and because she seemed to expect something else, he awkwardly patted her hand. Her skin was dry, almost papery, and he thought at once how old she looked there in the bed. Chronologically she wasn't, she'd had all her kids young, but it seemed her body's decline had sped past her. He didn't like the part of himself that instantly brightened at the realization she couldn't go on forever. But he didn't particularly hate it, either.

# CHAPTER SEVENTEEN

"**DO YOU REALLY** believe in it?" Nate blurted out. "Possession, I mean?"

Carrie paused behind her desk where she gathered the materials she'd need for the séance. They were in her home office, not at work, and Nate felt a tingle of nervous excitement being here. Carrie kept her home and professional lives strictly separate, and he wondered what it meant that she'd finally let him in. Was Aury right? Did he have a chance?

*She probably just didn't feel like driving across town twice. Stop being that guy.*

She tucked a small metal bowl and what looked like a wooden pestle into her bag, then turned to face him. "To an extent, although I don't think it happens the way people think it does."

He fidgeted near the door, running his thumb along the latch. "So there's no real chance something actually crawled inside her, shoved her in the backseat and made her do its bidding."

She tilted her head. "I've seen entirely too much to believe in any absolutes, so I won't say it's outright impossible. More things on heaven and earth, *et cetera*. If you're asking whether I've ever seen it work like that, the answer is no. Nothing even close."

He bit his lip and nodded, not meeting her eye.

"What about you?" she asked.

He frowned. "What about me?"

"You asked if I believed possession was real. What's your take?"

"You know what I think. It's all bullshit."

"I know what you *say*. But I get the impression there's more to that house than you're letting on. So what do you remember?"

He scoffed and fidgeted. "Just her. Doing her Stella shit, being awful and abusive. Hamming it up on this whole supernatural angle."

"So you never saw anything out there? No ghosts, nothing you couldn't explain?"

"How many times is someone gonna ask me that? No, there was nothing paranormal going on."

She stayed silent, seeing the lie for what it was, he imagined. She'd always been able to read him so well.

He sighed. "Honestly, I don't know anymore. I didn't think there was anything . . . but since we've been back . . . "

"Repressed memories?" she asked.

"Maybe. Or maybe just the power of suggestion, my mind creating images to match what Katy and Aury say." Yet that sense memory of being under the malodorous duvet, heart thumping in his ears, sheer terror as he watched a silhouette stand over them. The sight of Stella's shadow that seemed to wander on its own. The pacing footsteps on the third floor in the dead of night. And that sound . . . so impossible to place, yet stirring his dread in a way he didn't understand.

"I get it. It's hard to tell, and there aren't any foolproof ways of coaxing them to surface without risking additional suggestion taking root. But don't discount your experiences on their face. Don't close out an entire realm of explanation out of stubbornness."

"I won't. I'm not," he answered immediately. The knee-jerk need to do things perfectly, to meet her expectations without a learning curve.

She smiled, then cocked her head at him. "Want to tell me what's really worrying you?"

He crossed his arms, then shrugged. "No. Yes? I don't know. It seems so dumb."

Carrie lowered herself into the large easy chair behind her desk. He'd been surprised at the sight of it, expecting a standard office chair, something functional and sleek, but she'd smiled and said she always went for maximum comfort, given the chance. She crossed one knee over the other and waited.

He blew out a breath and moved toward a dark red microfiber couch against the far wall. He didn't like how much this felt like yet another therapy session—he didn't want that to be the nature of their relationship. But he had to know.

"I've been having these dreams. These really bad, vivid dreams, ever since I agreed to do the show."

She nodded. "Sleep paralysis again?"

He shuddered. "Yeah, the first night."

"Tell me."

As briefly as possible he filled her in, not meeting her eyes. "Katy's had them, too. And I'm sure it's coincidence, and they're not really the same anyway, but when Stella said that bit about the shadow . . . and the eyes. The blue-lit eyes."

Carrie picked up a pencil from her desktop and balanced it across the back of one hand. "And you had this dream *before* she told you this?"

He nodded, swallowed. "That combined with the sound . . . I don't know. I *don't* believe in possession. I'm not even always sure I believe in ghosts, no offense."

She smiled. "None taken. I'm still on the fence, myself."

He gave a bark of laughter. "Sure you are. Well, anyway. I just . . . it's bugged me, since then. I mean the dreams were bad enough, but wondering if we really saw and heard the same things . . . it makes it more real, doesn't it?"

She sat forward and put the pencil down. "Yes, but not in the sense of verifying true possession. The fact that you and your sister heard the same sound in your dreams, and that Stella described something similar to what you saw, it argues that these are pieces of your subconscious. Discarded bits of memories from a traumatic time in your life, manifesting now that it's all being stirred up. It's much more likely that the sound is something you all heard as children, as you suspected."

His gut dropped at her words, something dark trying to surface, but he couldn't catch it. Turned away from the memory.

"What's more likely than having heard Stella describe this shadow demon and internalizing it?" She stood, crossed the room to sit beside him on the couch. "You're not possessed, Nate."

He picked at his cuticles and wouldn't look at her.

"And I can tell you exactly why you dreamed what you did. Katy, too."

He looked up, annoyed at himself for the instant leap of hope in his heart.

"You told me your brother died by strangulation. Is that right?"

"Asphyxiation. His . . . his throat, it got all fucked up somehow, and he couldn't get any air." Nate shuddered, closed his eyes against the images that rushed to his head whenever he thought of his brother's death. His purpled face, bloodshot eyes, throat distended, tongue swollen and protruding. Clawing at his useless windpipe, struggling in agony to the very last. He'd never know if the visage he conjured was close to the mark or not—he'd never seen his brother's face again, once the door closed behind him, but Nate's imagination filled in the gaps based on what he'd overheard from whispering adults. "She claimed it was an accident. That he fell, or she pushed him, and he hit the corner of the desk just right," he rasped from a dry throat. "I've never seen the autopsy findings— they're sealed, I guess because there was an investigation. Or the appearance of one, anyway."

"Hit the desk? With his throat?" she asked, fetching

him a bottle of water from the mini fridge next to her chair and standing over him while he drank it. "And the wounds backed that up? No one questioned it?"

He drained a third of the water before trying to speak again. "*We* sure as hell did. But we didn't have anything to go on. They never told us specifics—just that he died because he couldn't get any air." He laughed harshly. "Tried to make it sound like a peaceful death, like going to sleep. Right. Because slowly dying from lack of oxygen is such an easy way to go."

"I'm very sorry, Nate. It's awful, not knowing. People often make the mistake of withholding information, especially from kids, thinking it will spare them. But it's generally better to know the truth, to sit with it." She settled on the couch again.

"That's what we wanted, all of us. Truth."

"But the manner of Shawn's death—it lends more credence to your nightmares being a result of shared memory, doesn't it?"

"Does it?"

"Think about it. You dreamed of choking, of having your airway blocked while something holds you down. You're reliving the trauma you're afraid your brother experienced before he died."

Nate straightened his shoulders and frowned. It made sense, but the way he felt in the dream . . . it didn't *feel* right. But what did he know? "And . . . the other stuff?"

"The other version of you, you mean?"

"I don't know if that's what it is—it's more like . . . something that takes the shape of me, then takes over."

She nodded, her gaze to one side as she considered. "And in your dream, you're fighting like hell against it, both the ingestion of the other, and the actions it takes once it's in control. It sounds like the terror stems from taking that evil into yourself, against your will."

He clenched his hands around the water bottle to keep them from shaking. "Like being possessed."

"If you want to see it that way, sure. The subconscious doesn't explain things clearly, I'm afraid. But from what I know of you, I believe the fear that's playing out has to do with *letting* it happen, letting it take control. Giving in to the desire to harm."

Nate looked up sharply. "That's not . . . I mean, I don't have some deep-seated desire to lose my shit and be a serial killer." He felt the shift of a lifetime of repressed fury and wondered how much she could see of the self he hid.

She smiled. "Not a serial killer, no, but you worry, don't you? About what you might be capable of if you lost control? Isn't that fear what's guided your life to this point? Guided all three of you? Now you learn your sister's violating that pact, daring to get close to people, some of them children. It makes sense that fear would come to the surface."

Nate's brow furrowed, but the tension in his gut eased a little. He'd been so focused on the eerie alignment of details, he hadn't looked at the dream itself, but it seemed painfully obvious now. "And that's why Katy's having similar dreams."

"Exactly. It's the same thing, just presented differently. She's about to join a family, embark on motherhood. It's natural she'd be nervous about it, especially because the children aren't abstract constructs, they're people she already knows and loves. What's more normal than a parent worried about screwing it up? We all have dreams like that, especially when we're new to it."

Nate blinked. "You have kids?"

She nodded but didn't otherwise address the fact she'd never discussed her family in all the years they'd worked together. No pictures in her office, no mention of leaving early to attend soccer practice. She wore no wedding ring so he'd always assumed she was on her own. Like him.

"The point is, you're all terrified of becoming your mother. You think that because you don't understand her behavior towards you as children, that because you couldn't predict her moods, that you wouldn't have any control over your own. Lots of children of narcissists feel that way, and a good percentage let it ruin their lives. Forget having a family, they never let *anyone* close to them."

Nate's face burned, thinking of Aury, so closed off. His own empty condo, each night spent alone. He'd long considered Carrie his closest relationship, but evidently he knew nothing about her.

Carrie patted his hand. "You're all missing the most important distinction."

He finally met her eyes. "What's that?"

"The fact that you give a shit about whether you're like her or not. You worrying you'll hurt other people already demonstrates how far removed you are from her. You think Stella ever worried about that for a second? How could she? Who else could there be to worry about, anyway? She's the only damn person in her world."

He didn't respond, wondering if he could trust what she was saying. If he could safely take comfort from it, or if he was setting himself up for more hurt.

She winked. "So suck it up, Lasco. You're just another dude with a crap childhood. No demons here."

She stood to finish packing her supplies, and he wished the good stuff was half as easy to believe as the bad.

# CHAPTER EIGHTEEN

**D**ESPITE HIS BEST EFFORTS to hurry the process along, it was dusk by the time they were once again settled into the horseshoe of soft chairs arranged on the second floor. This time Stella sat swathed in a plush blanket, her feet up on an ottoman that matched the rest of the set. It was weird seeing all this posh furniture, far nicer than the mismatched and damaged stuff they'd had as kids. He wondered how much money Aury had sunk into this little venture, including all of Helter's shiny new equipment.

Nate had spent half the afternoon while they waited on Stella pulling up old episodes of *The Cleaners!* and was surprised how low budget they were. Most of their shows were just the two guys creeping around ostensibly haunted locations, shouting and jumping at things that always happened off screen, endlessly asking, "Did you see that?"

If they managed to put together a decent episode from the Lasco shit show, that might change. There'd been a lot of local news coverage of Shawn's death at the time, most of it sensationalist garbage. For a few years, until Nate left the state for college, he'd barely been able to go in public without being recognized. Whispered about. It was a long time ago now, and people's memories were short, but he grimaced at the thought of it all being dragged up again. Probably no one would watch it—episodes of *The Cleaners!* had modest views. Hopefully the show would sink like a stone and stay out of the public eye.

Of course, if they got a confession on tape, that could change things, especially combined with everything else they'd already filmed. That noise, the fingers, that thumping last night—they'd had a camera on all of it. He frowned, watching Helter and Gunther as they moved around, getting equipment into position and fixing lighting. He believed Aury when she said she wasn't responsible for the things they'd experienced in the house, but that didn't mean it was supernatural. The guys could have planted all this shit—hell, who was in a better position to rig the place? Maybe not all of it—some things were too on point, too personal, with details they couldn't know. Last night, caught up in the moment, he'd been too afraid to question what he saw and heard, but now . . . he vowed to keep a closer eye on those two.

Carrie squeezed his shoulder. "Holding up okay?"

He shrugged and tried to smile, torn between a desire to impress her and his established need to be truthful. "I'll be better when this is over."

Her gaze went to Stella, soaking in the attention of Helter and both her daughters, Gunther keeping his distance behind the camera.

"I certainly hope so. I'd hate to leave you kids worse off than you already are."

*Kids.* His face twisted as his stomach dipped, but he told himself not to be an asshole. He could indulge his little crush on the boss until it faded, but only as long as he stayed grounded in reality. And there was no version of reality that resulted in them ending up together. Transference, like he'd told Aury. That's all it was, and heaven knows he'd seen enough of it. The deep disappointment he felt was a symptom of the same thing.

He noticed her looking at him again and flushed deeply, cleared his throat. "What are you worried about?" he asked in a low voice. "Ghost stuff?"

She frowned and cast a slow glance around the second floor. "Not entirely. There's energy here, like I said before.

A darkness, but again that could be more of the same, especially given what happened to your family here. Acts like that, pain like that, it leaves a mark. So it's possible we'll see something, maybe even a sentient manifestation."

The flesh on the back of Nate's neck crawled and he swiped a hand at the invisible cold that took hold of him. As much as he insisted he didn't believe, the possibility of seeing an actual ghost tonight, in this house of all places, was enough to give him the creeps. "Should we be worried?" he asked, wondering how the hell he could prepare for something like that.

Carrie shrugged. "It's likely to frighten us, if it's here and makes an appearance, but all we have to do is close the circle. I'm not concerned about that part."

"Then what?"

She returned to her study of his mother, unmoved when the other woman caught her staring and gave the most ludicrously over- the-top glare, jaw jutted out, eyes and brows narrowed. She looked like a three-year-old on the verge of a meltdown, and when Carrie didn't react, she sniffed and turned away.

Only then did his boss return her attention to him. "One of the biggest mistakes stable people make is believing they can predict and account for the thought patterns of narcissists."

His heart sunk. "You think this is a dumb idea."

She smiled. "Not by any means—it was quite clever of you, in fact, and there's a good chance we'll get something out of it. But it's dangerous to think we can predict what she'll do. The three of you have endured so much, worked so hard to get out from under her shadow, and the trauma of your brother's death. I just don't want to see you hurt again."

Warmth flooded through him but he ducked his head. "Doesn't seem like I've made much progress. I feel like I'm right back here as a teenager, with no control over any aspect of my life, at the mercy of whatever mood she swings into. I thought I'd done a better job than this."

She touched him again, waited until he met her eyes. "Nathan. It's not about building a high enough wall—it's about developing boundaries, and the tools to heal when people do horrible things to you. You may be backsliding at the moment, but none of the work you've done is wasted. Let's get you through today, and I'm betting you'll find the path back to peace is a lot smoother than you think."

He opened his mouth, to say what he didn't know, but Stella's shrill voice rang out and he was silenced.

"What the *hell* is this?" She held up a single piece of paper, rattling it in Helter's face. "You expect me to sign this garbage?"

The kid held up both hands, backed away a step. "Mrs. Lasco, it's a formality. Just a standard release, with um, boiler language."

Stella's anger grew, all three Lasco children flinching away from the coming storm. She leaned out of her chair and spoke in clipped, shaky tones. "Now you listen to me, young man. I'm not signing any piece of legalese bullshit just so you can say whatever you want about me, twist everything, take *my* tragedy and make it about something else. I—"

"Boiler*plate*," interrupted Carrie. "And the release isn't his, it's mine. Do you have a problem with some of the language?"

Helter backed away and joined Gunther on the other side of the room with an audible sigh of relief.

Stella, far from being appeased, ground her teeth together, eyes snapping as she focused on worthier prey. "*All* of it. I'm not signing away my rights so you can cover your ass. What kind of *professional* needs people to sign a waiver before they'll help?"

"All of them, I'd imagine," Carrie responded. "You've never signed a medical release? Or an engagement letter from your divorce attorney?"

The room darkened as though a shadow passed before the lamplight, and Nate again felt the brush of cold air at the back of his neck. Aury stood with one of her arms across her middle, a copy of the same release in her hand. She wasn't looking at him, but he noticed her shiver and pull her jacket tighter around herself. He wasn't imagining it—something was happening. He cast a narrowed glance at Helter and Gunther, but they hadn't moved, as far as he could tell.

"How *dare* you throw my divorce in my face? If you had any idea how hard it is, being a single mother, no help at all, and if I hadn't divorced their father we might *all* be dead. I stayed for them, and I left for them. That's true sacrifice, something someone like you will *never* understand."

The temperature dropped another few degrees and the shadows deepened. Nate wrinkled his nose against a whiff of an odd chemical scent, an odor like ozone. His heartbeat quickened. Every word of Carrie's reassurance fell away, and he froze in place.

Before Carrie could answer, the sound of the front door creaking open silenced everyone. Nate held his breath and Katy squeaked. They all stayed locked in a tableau until the door slammed back and Nate screamed. Thankfully no one heard him over Gunther's much louder, and apparently unabashed bellow.

No one spoke, the silence stretching Nate's nerves.

"Did you lock the front door?" hissed Aury, and Nate's gaze swiveled to Helter.

The kid licked his lips. "Of course I did, but listen, there's something—"

"Quiet," Aury said, raising a hand for silence.

There was the unmistakable thud and creak of a heavy weight being placed on the bottom stair. Katy moaned and Gunther went straight to her, putting himself between her and the top of the staircase. Aury stood still, listening, but Stella had gone completely white.

Nate set his shoulders and strode to the railing overlooking the first floor. All he could see was a shadow, stretching far up the steps, almost to the first landing. He swallowed against the nauseating certainty it was Stella's shadow, coaxed out of hiding now that the family was back to feed its dark appetites.

"Hey," he shouted, ignoring the dry break in his voice. "This is private property. Who the hell's down there? You've got about two seconds to answer me before I call the cops."

His words hung in the air for a long, agonizing heartbeat, and he strained his vision in the gloom, hoping like hell he wouldn't see the glow of that white t-shirt again.

"Nathan?" called a deep, male voice. He couldn't place it, but it plucked strings of memory from somewhere, and he leaned over the banister.

"Who's that?"

The footsteps resumed in answer to his question, and Nate scuttled backward.

"Don't shoot, I'm unarmed, kiddo."

For the briefest of moments, Nate's heart cracked in two. Was it Shawn after all? Had he appeared, more corporeal than any of them could have imagined?

Then a man stepped up from the shadows, his hands in the air. He was too big to be Shawn, and too old, not to mention too alive. Nate's heart plummeted to his stomach, then he sucked in a breath as he looked at the man. He squinted, recognition flickering somewhere in the back of his brain. *It can't be . . .*

"You," came Stella's voice from the other side of the room. It quivered with emotion Nate couldn't pin down. Fury? Hatred? Disgust?

"Hey there, Stella. It's been a long time."

The man's voice opened a closed door in Nate's subconscious. Warm memories rushed in, of a welcome change. Of a steadiness and a kindness that had been missing before he appeared in their lives, gone for good once he left.

Nate's mother surged from her chair and ran to the

man, throwing herself into his arms. Nate stared, mouth open, fighting the urge to do the same thing. The guy smiled at him over Stella's head.

"Mark?" squeaked Katy, moving out from behind Gunther. "Is it really you?"

The man turned and held a hand out to her. "Hey there, Katybug."

Nate made himself stay still, though he badly wanted to move to Mark. The man who, for an all too brief period, had been as close to a true father as the Lasco kids ever had. The only boyfriend who cared enough to stand up for them when the honeymoon period of oxytocin wore off and Stella reverted to her cruelties. Nate remembered trembling while Mark stood toe to toe with Stella, fear and hope warring in his young heart. No one had ever done that for them, not before or since, and Nate was annoyed to feel tears at the back of his eyes.

Mark's smile widened. "Nate. Man, did you ever grow up good. I'm so proud of you." He looked around the room, making steady eye contact. "Of all of you."

Swift footsteps approached, and Nate watched as Aury hurried over. For a brief moment he thought she'd throw herself on Mark as well, joining Katy and shoving Stella out of the way. Mark seemed to anticipate that, one arm opening wide to make room for her. He was therefore unprepared when Aury hauled back and clocked him, a spray of blood from his nose spattering Aury's face and Stella's hair.

"Owed you that," she said, then went back to her chair, not bothering to wipe the blood from her eyes.

# CHAPTER NINETEEN

**"I**T'S NOT BROKEN," said Carrie, straightening and handing the bloody wad of paper towels back to Mark. "Put some ice on it, though—you're likely to have a couple black eyes."

Mark sat in Stella's abandoned chair, eyes watering, his gray t-shirt covered in a bib of blood. Stella hovered at his side, trembling with rage, her eyes narrowed to slits, her mouth pursed in a way her children knew meant trouble.

"What the *hell* were you thinking, Aury? How *dare* you attack this man—do you have any idea how much he contributed to your welfare after your father left us?" Each word was bitten off rather than spoken, spittle flying from Stella's lips. It set Nate's stomach roiling, but Aury remained impassive.

"Thought you didn't have any support," she said, her jaw set.

"I also really can't keep track of whether your father left, or she left, or who divorced who," murmured Carrie in Nate's ear.

"Neither can we," he returned.

"No, Stella, I deserved it. She has every right to be pissed at me," said Mark, sounding a lot more nasal. He smiled gingerly around his injury and winced. "Just wish I'd remembered about that right hook. It was always pretty righteous."

Stella whirled on him, mouth open. "Deserved it? Why,

what did you ever do to her?" When he didn't answer, she looked back at her daughter. "Well?"

Mark held Aury's gaze, then sighed.

"He left," she said, her flat delivery a stark contrast to Stella's alt.

"That was a *grown-up* decision between us that had nothing to do with you children. If anyone has a right to be upset, it's me."

Mark opened his mouth, glanced at Aury then shut it again.

Aury glared. "You have no right to be here. You're not *supposed* to be here."

Mark's smile only touched one side of his mouth. "Maybe not, but I had to come. No way I was gonna leave you kids hanging. Not again."

Nate stepped into the breach. "Can someone please tell me what the hell's going on? What's he doing here?"

"I came here to fulfill a promise," said Mark in a low voice. "And I have a name, son."

Nate didn't respond. His first warm feelings toward the man had cooled off quick in the wake of Aury's assault. The memory of that blissful time when he was in their lives, easily the safest and most peaceful he'd ever felt as a child, was tainted with the confused grief of his leaving, and the spiral it sent Stella into. Maybe it was unfair to put so much on the guy, but Nate couldn't help how he felt. The older he'd gotten, the more immersed in his training, the more he realized how fucked up it was that no adult before Mark ever stepped in to stop what was going on. Even then, he didn't talk to the kids about it, and the safety net he represented left when he did. Hell, just someone taking them aside and saying hey, this is fucked up and you don't deserve it, that would have gone a long way toward righting the ships of their fucked-up psyches. Instead Mark left when they were most vulnerable. Hightailed it to get free of Stella, without considering what that meant for her children. Nate had tried hard to convince Carrie and everyone else it hadn't hurt, that he hadn't minded being abandoned, but it was bullshit.

Helter stepped forward, his Adam's apple bobbing up and down. "I, uh, I asked him here."

Nate turned on him slowly, his eyes wide, struggling to keep his anger in check. "Is this Jerry fucking Springer? What in the flying fuck does some ex-boyfriend of Stella's have to do with what happened to Shawn?" He glared at Mark. "You were long gone by then, so what the hell makes you think you have anything to say about *any* of this?"

Helter sunk his head between his shoulders, backpedaling weakly. "Look, he was there for the first part of everything that happened in the house. You guys were kids, and Stella—Mrs. Lasco, I mean—wasn't fully in her right mind. It seemed like a good idea to have another adult perspective from back then . . . "

Carrie touched Nate's shoulder and spoke in a low voice, only for his ears. "It's a distraction. All of this is a distraction—the shit with the waiver, this guy showing up—it's misdirection. Don't fall for it."

Breathing hard, he closed his eyes and nodded, tried to pull calm back around himself like he did with his patients. The room was still a babble of competing voices, accusations and incredulity doing the rounds punctuated by a healthy number of f-bombs. Carrie frowned and jerked her head, and he followed in her wake.

She stopped by the front window of the house, only a small section in the top left broken through, but it let in a bitter chill from the winter air outside.

"What's up?" he asked, hoping he sounded like something other than a raged-out lunatic.

"Did you notice the lights, when Stella got angry? The way the temperature dropped?"

He glanced back at his mother, nodded. "Yeah. And I swear I smelled something . . . "

"Like what?"

He shrugged. "Kind of . . . not quite a burning smell, but more of a . . ." he fumbled, reached for the word.

"Charge?"

He nodded. "Yeah, I guess."

She gestured to the nearest dark corner. "Logical explanation for that."

Nate squinted, frowned when he saw the squat little machine tucked out of sight, a single blue light glowing on the top. "What is that?"

"Air purifier. They're all over the place. Battery-powered."

He blinked. "Oh. That wasn't here before. I guess . . . did they do that for Katy? Because of the dust, and her asthma?"

She waggled a hand. "Maybe. That's one explanation, but I'm worried there's another."

"Which is what?"

"These machines act as ionizers. They put out positive ions—which, yes, can help clean the air, but they're also used in ghost hunting. They're thought to increase the energy for spirits to manifest, raise the odds of seeing something."

Nate frowned. "I guess that makes sense . . . doesn't it?" he asked when her expression didn't change.

"I don't like that those guys didn't mention it—they seem like they've been hidden. I don't think we were supposed to see them."

"So it's a trick, then? They're planning to fake something?"

She shook her head. "It's not a trick. At least, I don't see how they could be used that way, but I'm not an expert. I'm wondering what else they might be using without telling us. There are methods . . . machines and gizmos thought to up the intensity of paranormal encounters."

"Do they really work? I mean, is that something they can do?"

Carrie lifted a shoulder. "I don't use them myself—my

goal is to clear unwelcome energy, not stir it up. But there are professionals I know and trust who swear by methods like this."

Nate looked over at Helter, pushing buttons on his tablet, his gaze drawn to the third floor every so often. Was that because he knew something? Had he rigged something else to happen? Or just a result of their encounter the night before?

"So what does it mean, if they're using this kind of stuff?"

She frowned, her full lips pursed, dark eyes scanning from left to right as she thought it through. "Honestly? I'm not sure, but I don't like it. Whatever might be here, it doesn't need help. I don't want it getting any stronger— Stella will take care of that on her own."

Nate's face went cold. "You think . . . are you saying there's really something to this? The possession or whatever? Did Stella do that stuff with her mind?"

Carrie shook her head. "Not her mind: her emotions. I see it a lot. You wouldn't believe the power of uncontrolled human emotion, the effect it can have on the physical environment. And that woman has a *lot* of unchecked rage. In a way, I'm glad that Mark guy showed up—it redirected her, distracted her from channeling everything at me. It's likely the only reason things didn't get worse."

"Worse," he said. "You're kinda worrying me here, boss."

Her gaze snapped to his, her brows pulled together. "I'm not your boss, Nate, and if you can't stop thinking of me like that, we're going to have a problem."

He raised his hands. "Sorry, sorry. I'm on edge," he excused himself, wondering what it meant that she gave a shit.

*Fuck, is there any time you're not focused on your dick, you asshole?*

Her brow cleared. "I understand. Sorry for snapping." She stood on tiptoe to peer over his shoulder at the group

143

behind them. "I'm concerned because I'm not sure how far she can manipulate the physical environment. She doesn't have control of herself—there's no guaranteed way to bring her back down, settle the session if it gets rough. And if machines like those are helping things along, including her own capacity for influencing the environment, this could get very bad."

Nate thought of whirlwinds of unpredictable anger. The way the house felt when Stella got home, shadows seeming to pass over every source of light. The dread in his heart when he heard her car pull in the drive, the way they all held their breaths against whatever version of Stella would walk through the door. And if his barely glimpsed memories had any truth to them, if his sisters were right, then the horrors that had stalked the Lasco kids through long nights without hope of reprieve—whatever was there, it was conjured by their mother. The thought of it happening again, even as a fully grown man, made him sick to his stomach. "Okay, so let's turn them off. Make Helter tell us what else he's using so we can nix those, too. You're right, she doesn't need any outside assistance to make this shit happen."

Carrie frowned as she scanned the dim room, then sighed. "I agreed to do this assuming it would be a placebo of sorts, a way to draw your mother out, give her the spotlight she wants and prod her to tell the truth you three think you need. Now that we're here, I'm not sure this is a good idea. I'm not set up or prepared for a true cleansing, not the way I do them."

He licked dry lips and tried not to let his disappointment show. "And what would you need to do that part? A full one? Is there more stuff we need to get?"

"It's not so much supplies as it is preparation. When I'm asked in for a cleaning, I start with an analysis, to pin down where the problem originates. I have one-on-one and group sessions with the family members. I go through the whole family history, so I know what I'm getting into, and what I can use against it."

Nate frowned. "Against *it*?"

She held his gaze. "Yes, it."

"I don't understand, I thought all that shit that happens, all the stuff you 'clean,' that it's not anything but feelings out of control. You're telling me there's an intelligence to it?"

She nodded. "Sometimes. Often, even. I mentioned that before—a sentient presence."

"Right but . . . I thought it was still like . . . what do you call it, a revenant? Like the emotional energy, just . . . more," he finished lamely.

She raised an eyebrow. "That's not what sentience means though, is it?"

Nate sighed. "No. I know it's not."

"But that kind of thing is harder to wrap your mind around. I get it. I thought I was prepared, but the first time I came up against one . . . " Her gaze dropped and she rubbed at her arm, an unconscious gesture. "Anyway. They're not as common, but they do occur. And sometimes they don't have any intention of leaving." Her eyes narrowed and she took a step back, the worry on her brow smoothing as her face settled into her normal, *I've got this handled* expression. "Aury," she said.

Nate turned to find his sister at his shoulder, arms wrapped tight around herself, attention on Carrie.

"This doesn't change anything," she said. "Him showing up—it doesn't matter. We're still doing this."

Carrie didn't answer.

Aury turned her gaze on Nate, her jaw set in stone. "We're doing this. Now."

He found nothing to go on in Carrie's blank expression. "We were talking about what happened before Mark got here. The lights, the cold. We're worried this is more of an actual, um, haunting or whatever, than we realized."

Aury rolled her eyes. "Of course it is. Everyone but you gets that, Nate." She looked at Carrie again. "So, what? That's what you do, isn't it? Why you're here?"

Carrie sighed. "In part, yes. I'm here to help Stella reach the point of confession, for your sake. Last night, with only four of us, this place felt pretty harmless. Dark, and stained with turmoil, but mostly inert. Now that Stella's here, it feels different. Seething, almost."

Nate thought how accurate a term that was, seething. The way most communication was delivered, through clenched teeth, eyes hard and narrowed, cruelties seeping out from between tightened lips. He shuddered.

Aury shrugged. "So? How's that different from other cases you've worked? They can't have all been harmless, or people wouldn't call you in."

Carrie smiled briefly. "True. But there's a lot of preparation that goes into it—weeks, even months sometimes. We don't have that here."

Aury stiffened, and Nate could almost feel the anger roll off her, thinking Carrie's theory about emotion affecting the environment wasn't that far-fetched. Aury didn't let it out as he expected, instead looking back at their younger sister. Katy's chair was pulled up close to Mark's, and she held his hand while she talked. Her shoulders were straighter, her eyes shining. Stella looked less than pleased, but what else was new?

Aury sighed and stepped closer to Carrie, lowered her voice. "Katy doesn't have weeks or months to wait. She shouldn't have to—she's been waiting her whole damn life to have a family, and now she has the chance."

Carrie's expression softened. "I know, and it's not that I don't want to help."

"You don't know her like we do," Aury said. "Those dreams she's been having? They're fucking with her, a lot. She's not sleeping, she's miserable. I'm afraid of what she might do if we leave this hanging."

Nate's body went cold, fear like a frozen wave knocking into him. "You think she might do it again?"

Aury shrugged. "I don't know. I hope not—she never brings me that far into her confidence, so I don't really know where her head's at. What I do know is, right now she has a reason to hope. But what if her fiancé gets tired of waiting? What if she falls back into old patterns and drives him out of her life? If we take that hope away . . . "

Carrie glanced between them. "Your sister's attempted suicide before?"

Nate nodded, swallowing hard. "It's been years, and she was in a really bad place. She's always struggled with depression, and it just . . . caught up with her, I guess." The years didn't diminish the hopeless terror he'd felt when he found his little sister, unresponsive on the floor of the shitty apartment she'd lived in at the time. The froth of vomit on blue lips, her breath so shallow he couldn't tell at first if she was still alive. The bottle of over-the-counter pain meds empty at her side. Worst of all, the despair on her face when she woke up in the hospital, still inhabiting a life that had become too much for her.

"I'm not trying to manipulate you," said Aury softly. "None of that's on you, our family history, whatever. I'm just telling you the risks as I see them."

Carrie looked at Nate. "Your dreams, too."

He shrugged uncomfortably. "Well yeah, I mean they're not pleasant, but I'm not actually at risk or anything." Except for the drinking. The bottles of whiskey and scotch he carried everywhere now, the cabinet full of bottom shelf shit because he couldn't afford to plow through the good stuff like he had been. He might not swallow a bottle of pills, but he was back to killing himself slowly, as he'd done for years before straightening out.

Carrie closed her eyes briefly and sighed. "Okay. We'll give it a try. It's not like an exorcism anyway, not like we can make things worse. I might just fail."

Aury reached out and gripped the other woman's arm. "You won't. Not with us here. You get it started, and we'll see it through." She cleared her throat and let go. "Thank you. You have no idea what this means to us."

Carrie met his gaze and held it for several seconds, and

he wondered what she expected him to say. Should he stop it? Side with Carrie and insist on a longer preparation period? But he didn't want to. He wanted to deal with this here, now, not commit to months of agonized uncertainty.

Before he made up his mind on what to say, Carrie gestured for Aury to precede her. When his sister was out of hearing range, she leaned close. "Turn off every ionizer you can find." The intensity in her voice made him wary, and he hurried to comply, checking every room on the second floor while Carrie gave her instructions to everyone else. When he was sure he'd gotten them all, he found his seat and gave her a thumbs up.

She nodded and went to the open spot at the other end of the horseshoe. "Are we ready to begin?"

# CHAPTER TWENTY

**T**HERE WAS LITTLE window dressing to Carrie's process. No spells, no spirit board or crystal ball, just a couple of breathing exercises for calm and focus. The room was dark, despite Helter's argument for better lighting. Aury won him over, talking up the atmosphere of a séance lit only by candles. It was cold, but since the utilities weren't turned on that didn't mean anything. The eeriest part for Nate was the silence. He looked around the circle like a kid peeping during the blessing, and everyone's mouths were closed, their eyes on Carrie. Helter had joined Gunther behind the camera and was chewing on a thumbnail, still casting glances at the third floor when he thought no one was looking.

Carrie struck the little brass bowl they'd retrieved from her house and a gong sounded, humming with resonance. Her clear voice rang out into the heavy atmosphere. "Tell me what you remember, Stella. Take us back to that night."

Nate frowned. He'd expected an intro of some kind, a summoning of the spirits, a call to whatever might reside inside his mother. Inside himself. Would Stella even bother with the truth if she couldn't hide behind a supernatural persona? He felt for his brother's knife, cold and comforting in his pocket. One way or another, she'd tell them what they wanted to know.

Stella sat straighter in her chair, stared into the darkness at the center of their circle. "It was angry that night," she said in a softer voice than any her children had heard her use. "It made me feel restless, antsy. Like if I didn't do something to appease it, I would crawl out of my own skin."

Nate shuddered. *Appease it*. He remembered her pacing around the downstairs that night, barking orders and taking jabs. They were all cleaning the house though it was past time for them to be in bed. They had school in the morning, but Stella refused to listen to their protests. Whenever one of them thought they were through, she'd come marching over, sneering at the job and demanding they do it over again. Had the shadow been there then? Had it smiled with too-long teeth as it watched from the dark with nothing eyes?

As they worked, she'd picked at them, saying what she knew must get under their skins. Although really, Nate wasn't sure she *did* know. He didn't understand her compulsion to hurt, and tried to recall if it had ever been quite like that before they'd moved here. It bothered him that he couldn't remember, but the years before had receded into an uneasy haze.

"I tried to keep busy cleaning, and I kept the kids with me instead of sending them to bed."

"Why?" asked Carrie. "Wouldn't they have been safer out of reach of whatever was making you feel that way?"

Stella narrowed her gaze. "I was afraid it would get out again. It was bad that night, worse than ever, and I thought if it got loose, I wouldn't be able to control it, keep it from hurting them. I was trying to protect them."

A loud beep sounded from something just outside the circle, an instrument of some kind, and everyone but Stella and Carrie jumped. Helter leaned over his equipment, eyes wide, his face lit by madly blinking red and green lights. "There's something here," he whispered, making Nate's flesh creep.

Carrie took no notice, her focus on Stella. Nate told himself he imagined the movement of hair by her face, as though a breeze blew past her. "That had happened before?

It separated from you, was able to do things independent of you?"

Stella shrugged, looked away. "It must have. Sometimes when I woke up, things would be different. Moved around, or messed up when I'd just cleaned it."

Nate met Aury's gaze. He couldn't remember their mother ever cleaning anything, only standing over them while they did so.

"I thought the kids were doing it at first, to upset me."

"And that was something that happened as well?" Carrie asked evenly.

Stella shot her a glare, her lips pursing. The gizmo beeped again, several times in succession. "Yes, of course it did. I had four teenagers—you'd know if *you* were a mother. All they do is look for ways to upset you. Everything they do is about pushing your buttons."

"Can you give me an example?"

Stella rolled her eyes. "I can give you a hundred."

"Just one will do."

Stella fumed and fidgeted, crossing and uncrossing her legs. Buying time while she fabricated proof. "Well, they hated me dating. Especially Aury." She shot a vicious look at her eldest daughter and again the air seemed different, almost crackling with static electricity.

Nate's nails dug into his thighs and he struggled to stay silent.

"What makes you say that?"

"Whenever I had a date, she'd misbehave. Refuse to listen to me, get rebellious. Pick a fight all so I wouldn't be happy."

"Name one fucking time," growled Nate. There was definitely air movement, now, fanning his heated cheeks. Helter's machine gave off strings of beeps, one right after the other, but they all ignored it this time. A storm was rising and Nate wanted it to break over their heads. "Give us one clear example of Aury doing that."

Aury waved him off and the beeps died down. "It

doesn't matter. I'm sure I was horrible at all times—we don't need to rehash."

Stella couldn't seem to decide whether to be grateful, triumphant or livid at Aury's interruption. The expressions chased themselves across her face like it was a slot machine, and the ridiculousness of it brought Nate's anger down. He could almost feel sorry for her, if she wasn't so goddamn awful.

"Tell us about that night," Aury said. "Tell us what happened to Shawn."

A candle guttered as the chill breeze rose again, stronger this time. *This is really fucking happening.*

Helter squeaked as it ruffled his hair visibly, almost like fingers parting it. Another alarm went off, this one higher and steady, and he grinned at Gunther, showing him the tablet. Fear forgotten in his excitement. Nate watched Gunther's expression change when he dropped his gaze from the camera. The big man's brows went up, then quickly snapped together. "Dude, that reading is crazy high," he said in a low voice.

"I know, man—I told you this place was the real deal."

Gunther opened his mouth but Helter motioned for him to lift the camera again. "I don't want to miss a thing— keep it rolling."

"Stella?" said Carrie. "Did you hear Aury?"

Stella glared at Carrie and Aury in turn, looked ready to argue, but Mark reached out and took her hand. She melted, giving him a blinding smile and patting his hand back. Wriggled in her seat and sat back.

"Shawn was being his usual self that night. Smart mouthed, disrespectful. Trying to pick a fight, like always. I tried to be patient, but *it*, the thing inside me, it didn't care. It wanted out, and it wanted to shut him up."

Katy caught her breath on a soft sob and Nate wrapped an arm around her shoulders. Lined up between his sisters, listening to Stella spin a new reality. It was an uncomfortably familiar feeling.

Carrie leaned forward. "Is that what it said to you? Did it speak inside your head, or was it more of a feeling it conveyed?"

Stella kneaded her hands in her lap, looking everywhere but at the other woman's face. "Both. Sometimes it was this voice—this low, gravelly voice that would grind in my head, telling me what it wanted me to do." She swallowed hard, glanced at her children before dropping her gaze again.

Nate's gut shifted, a thick crawling feeling moving through it. *It's not real. She's full of shit—there was no ghost or whatever that came for her, which means there's no way one came for you. A dream, only a dream.*

"What . . . what did it look like?" Katy asked in a breathy voice.

Stella rolled her eyes. "I hardly see how that matters."

Katy dropped her gaze to her lap without answering, but Nate understood. Was it the same thing they'd seen in their dreams? The same thing he'd seen lurking in every still place in this house? No matter how loudly he insisted it wasn't real, he wanted to know, too.

Carrie inclined her head. "Right now everything matters. We're getting it all out there, aren't we? So why don't you tell her?"

Stella sighed, fussed with the collar of her shirt, pulled at the waistline of her pants. "It wasn't always the same."

"Okay. Why don't you start with how it first appeared to you?"

Stella looked up at the ceiling and her voice took on a dreamy quality. "At first it was just . . . a person. Like any other person. And it didn't scare me. In fact I welcomed it—it was another adult, someone I could talk to. Share the burden."

Nate's stomach turned and he fought the urge to glance behind him. He wished he'd asked Carrie about safety parameters—were they not supposed to look outside the circle of the séance? What if one of them broke the connection, would they all be doomed?

"And it didn't scare you, finding a stranger in the house?"

"No. It didn't feel like a stranger—it felt like someone I'd known who'd been gone a long time. I was . . . comfortable with it."

Carrie's expression didn't so much as twitch. "Where were you when you first saw it?"

"Upstairs. The third floor. He was sitting in the office up there, behind my desk. His back was to the door, but I could tell his shoulders were broad, strong. He had nice hair."

Nate frowned. Stella's haunting took the form of an attractive man? That didn't line up with anything he'd seen. Where was the heavy shadow she claimed haunted her room? The dark presence that paced the house and scared her? The strange blue-lit eyes? Who was this guy they'd never heard of?

"Could you see his face?" Carrie asked.

Stella laughed, a girlish sound. Fuck, she'd had a crush on this thing, hadn't she?

"Not really. At first I couldn't get the right angle. His back was always to me, but he knew where I was, even without being able to see me. His voice was always directed right at me, and closer than he really was. It felt . . . intimate."

Disgust lifted Nate's upper lip, and he wondered where his empathy was. If it were anyone else in the world, he'd have been afraid for them, afraid of the unknown entity taking advantage of a vulnerable, lonely person.

Stella continued, still sounding dreamy. "Later . . . he'd look at me, but his face was kind of . . . fuzzy. Out of focus. I could never really make it out. But it didn't matter to me. He was so kind. So admiring—he saw all the things about me no one else paid attention to. He saw me as more than just a mother, or a wife. He saw me as a woman."

Bile rose in Nate's throat and he hoped they weren't about to be treated to a tale of ghost smut. At least not one

154

involving his mother. He looked around the circle and realized Helter's gizmos had gone silent, the lights no longer blinking. His stomach sank. She wasn't going to tell them anything real. She'd done it again. Built up their hopes, even his, and he'd thought he was immune to that kind of thing. Self-hatred filled him at his idiocy.

"So you spent a lot of time with it?" Carrie prodded.

"Him," corrected Stella sharply, before returning her gaze upward, apparently unaware of her contradictions. Minutes before the thing had been an *it*, but not anymore. "Yes, I did. I didn't have anyone else to talk to—everyone abandoned me after my divorce. Their father lied, told people untrue things about me, so they cut me out of their lives. Even my own brother. And the women." She threw her head back and laughed, putting a hand to her cleavage, unsubtly adjusting her neckline downward. "They just couldn't stand the idea of a single woman around their men, so they ostracized me, too."

"But not the . . . entity," said Carrie, and Nate wondered how she managed to keep a straight face. Bored and annoyed, he let his gaze travel around the room again.

"No, not him. We started spending a lot of time together. He'd watch movies with me, sometimes we'd sit up and talk. He made me laugh."

Nate's stomach responded again and he pressed a hand to it. All at once he remembered hearing her laugh in the dead of night. He'd thought she was talking to herself, or maybe on the phone, and the idea she'd been cozying up to some imaginary suitor made him queasy.

"And when did he stop coming?" asked Carrie.

The little grin slid from Stella's face in slow motion, her expression hardening. "What are you talking about?"

Carrie cocked her head. "From what I understand, you spoke about a heavy shadow in your room. Something that scared you. That doesn't sound like what you're describing, so I'm asking when it changed."

Stella dropped her chin to look at Carrie, and Nate

flinched at the empty, dead-eyed stare. "I don't remember exactly. He started looking different. Subtle changes at first, getting hazier all the time. And then one night he wasn't there anymore. He'd been replaced by someone else."

Helter's machine beeped again, louder this time, more frantic. Gunther looked grim behind the camera, but Helter was almost dancing in place.

"Replaced by what?"

"It was hard to tell at first. It was blurry, like at the beginning. But then, after a while, I realized it was a woman."

"And did you recognize her?" asked Carrie.

Stella looked down at the floor, her voice going flat. "No. Sometimes I thought she was familiar, but then others . . . .she was a stranger. And her face was . . . bloody. Her upper lip was torn somehow, not in the right place. Her skin hung oddly, and her eyes . . . "

The beeping increased in intensity, the heavy pressure feeling of a coming storm picking up again. Nate didn't know what the beeping was supposed to mean, but it probably wasn't good. He had the uneasy urge to stop the session, to pull back from the precipice.

"That sounds scary," observed Carrie.

Stella frowned. "It wasn't, somehow. I didn't even notice after a while. And she helped me, too, even more than the man. Gave me advice, told me what to do."

*Advice?* None of this was lining up with what she'd said in the previous session. Yesterday she'd made it sound like she was a victim, that the same thing haunted them all. What the hell was this? Multiple entities, hanging out and giving advice? Where was the possession aspect? How did Stella plan to get herself off the hook? He looked around the circle, wondering if anyone else had noticed.

Carrie kept on. "So she's the one who was giving you instructions that night? The night Shawn died?"

Stella raised her eyes briefly, no longer empty. She smiled. "Yes. My helper. My friend."

Katy's breath got thin and she pressed closer to Nate. Aury was still as stone on his other side.

*Friend?*

"And what did your friend tell you that night?"

"She . . . she wanted me to make Shawn sorry. To set an example for the others, so they wouldn't make the same mistakes." She leaned forward, eyes bright and intent on Carrie. "You have to understand, I *had* to make him mind, all of them. If they didn't, if they sassed or disobeyed me, she would get angry. She didn't like it when they talked back, when they made me feel bad. She told me it wasn't right, that it was my job to keep them in line. Discipline is the *only* way with kids like that. She'd seen it before—said she'd helped other families before ours."

Other families? What the hell did that mean?

"And you agreed with her methods? You didn't see anything wrong with what she proposed?"

Stella scowled. "She only wanted to help me. She knew what Shawn was—knew how dangerous he'd be if left unchecked. She didn't want to see us end up like the last family."

The skin crawled on Nate's neck. "What last family? Who are you talking about?"

She moved her gaze to him slowly and he wished he'd kept quiet. Her lips turned up at the edges. "The ones who died here. They saw the dark, too."

Carrie spoke again and Stella looked away from Nate. "Can you tell me about this family?"

Stella shrugged. "I'm sure the boys can fill you in. You did all the research before we started, didn't you?"

Helter frowned. "No. I mean yes, we did, but we never found any record of something like that."

"Are you calling me a liar?" asked Stella, her voice tight and frigid.

"No, that's not what I mean, I only—"

"Because I wouldn't take kindly to that."

She held Helter with her gaze for seconds that

stretched into eternity, until Carrie came to the rescue again.

"Tell me what happened with Shawn that night."

Katy's shoulders trembled under Nate's arm, and he breathed deep, counting. His own anger was up again, crawling through his veins like an army of fire ants, unwanted memories of his helplessness rolling through him. His body hummed with tension—sitting still was killing him. Aury reached out and took his free hand, held it in a death grip.

"All I meant to do was teach him a lesson. Get him to understand that he had to obey me, implicitly and without question, if he wanted to stay safe."

"Was that why you hit him with the bat?"

Aury's voice was unexpected, breaking into Carrie's rhythm, but if it bothered her she didn't show it. Stella turned toward her daughter slowly.

"Excuse me, young lady?"

Aury sat forward, crushing Nate's hand in hers. "You're making it sound like things got out of hand through no fault of your own. But that's not true. You hit him. After you lined us all up, you were holding that bat, the metal one. And when Shawn didn't do what you wanted, you hit him with it. Was that for his safety, too?"

The memory came swirling back in full force. It filled his ears and eyes, the sudden, violent movement of the bat, drawn back briefly before connecting with Shawn's face right between the eyes. There had been a meaty thud, one that resonated though Nate's bones, as though he could feel the impact himself. He'd looked at his mother, the last time he'd thought of her that way, but there was no one behind those eyes anymore, if there ever had been. Cold gripped him from all sides as the thought came, unbidden, that there really was something else in control that night.

*No. Don't let her dodge responsibility. Stella did this, all of it. She bashed her own son with a fucking aluminum bat.*

Shawn had swayed at the impact, his eyes crossed, mouth sagging to one side. They'd all felt the ground shift beneath them, with the new knowledge of what Stella was capable of. She had no boundaries anymore, no bright line they could tell themselves she wouldn't cross. Anything at all could happen, and the remembered dread of that night clutched Nate's gut with a hand of ice.

They'd all held their breaths, waiting for Shawn to slump to the ground, dazed or dead. Instead he'd focused his gaze, straightened his shoulders and lowered his chin. His fists clenched at his sides, he'd loomed over Stella, ignoring the blood running down his face. "Try it again," he'd said in a voice that didn't sound like his. Or was Nate only remembering it that way in light of everything that happened after? Surely his brother hadn't changed in that moment, the room hadn't darkened, and Shawn hadn't looked at Stella with nothing eyes. Had he?

The machine was letting off a single endless beeping tone now, and Helter crept closer, leaned in to talk to Carrie. "Something wants to make contact."

A prickle of gooseflesh crept up Nate's spine, an uneasiness taking hold. Katy trembled beside him and Carrie met his gaze. She raised a brow, and he knew she'd do whatever he said in that moment. She'd stop it right there if he indicated, and they could all back away from this before something happened none of them could take back. They'd be no better off than before, but also no worse, and maybe that was all they could strive for. He looked at his sisters and wondered which choice would disappoint them more. Surely Katy had seen enough to believe what she needed to. Enough to convince herself her mother hadn't murdered her brother, that some haunting had.

But if he stopped them now, they'd never know. Never hear Stella's confession of what she did to Shawn, the missing member of their tribe. The shadow who was always there—not in the form of a ghost, but as an aching absence. Nate could tell himself he'd moved past all of this, set his eyes on a future outside of Stella's influence, but he saw it for the lie it was. He hadn't moved past anything, he'd only avoided it. Aury was the same, and he wanted more for her. Friends, a life, love. Happiness. She deserved it even if he didn't. So he took a breath and nodded at Carrie. *Let's finish this bitch.*

Her expression didn't indicate approval or disappointment, she only turned back to Stella and straightened her posture, sitting forward in the chair. Carrie closed her eyes, settled her hands on her thighs and took a breath. When she opened them again, she seemed different. Distant, somehow, like she'd ascended somewhere Nate couldn't follow.

"I'm speaking now to the consciousness responsible for the death of Shawn Lasco," she said in a low, ringing voice. "If you're here, please make yourself known."

Nate frowned, saw that Stella hadn't reacted. This wasn't what he'd expected—Carrie had been so close to a confession without resorting to woo woo ghost shit. Why was she redirecting now?

The gizmo beeped several times, then paused, then beeped again, the same pattern. Helter cleared his throat. "It's . . . we have to give it instructions. Tell it how to communicate using the box. It's pressure that makes it go off—all it has to do is touch it."

Carrie nodded, gestured for him to speak.

Helter coughed and straightened, attempting to imitate Carrie's mien. "Are you the spirit who killed Shawn Lasco? Beep once for yes, twice for no."

There were two swift beeps, then the machine fell silent. Nate's palms sweated, his breath coming fast.

Helter looked at a loss for a moment, then he spoke again. "Are you a spirit that died in this house?"

*Beep.*

Helter looked over his shoulder, rubbed his arms. "Uh, are you the, uh, someone who lived here before? A member of another family who died here?"

*Beep beep.*

"Are you Shawn?" Nate said before he could talk himself out of it.

*Beep.*

Tears filled Nate's eyes, surprising in their intensity. A wave of grief rolled through him and he fought the urge to collapse into tears. There would be time for that later.

"Shawn," whispered Katy beside him, her shoulders shaking with sobs.

"Do you want to tell us something, Shawn?" asked Carrie softly.

*Beep.*

"You can't listen to anything he says," Stella snarled. The dreamy quality of her voice had dropped, a frenetic urgency taking its place. Her gaze was locked on the beeping gizmo, lips curled past her teeth. "He's a liar."

*Beep beep.*

"You've had your turn," said Carrie with steel in her voice. "It's time to let Shawn speak."

Nate had never heard that tone from her before. He liked it.

"How do we . . . " Katy faltered. "How do we do this with only yes or no questions?"

Helter started to answer but Carrie cut him off.

"Are you here to tell us what happened that night?"

*Beep beep.*

Nate frowned. No?

"Are you here so you can be set at rest?" Carrie asked.

*Beep beep.* Red lights lit up Helter's other equipment.

"Then what?" asked Aury.

Nate shook his head. "He can't answer like that, it has to be—"

The beeps went shrill, continuous again, the red lights flashing brighter and stronger. Heavy wind swept through the room, and the bedroom doors down the darkened hallways slammed open one by one. There was no blaming it on a draft from the broken windows—whatever it was, it originated here, in the room with them. Everyone screamed save Stella and Carrie, still locked in silent battle. Stella seethed, panting between gritted teeth. Carrie held her gaze while she spoke to the dead.

"Are you here to warn us?" she asked.

*Beep.*

Stella's voice came again, a furious growl. "I fucking *told* you, he can't be trusted. Obey your mother and stop this now, Shawn Lasco."

Rage filled Nate and he pushed to his feet, fists clenched, trembling. "You don't get to tell him what to do, ever again."

She turned her molten gaze on him and he felt it like a furnace blast. The air around her shifted and Nate struggled to hold his ground.

"You didn't learn anything from all this, did you?" she asked, and her low, deadly tone made his skin crawl.

"I learned enough," he said with as much calm as he could muster. "I learned you only have the power over us that we give you. We're not kids anymore."

She lowered her chin, keeping her eyes on his. "Kid or not, I can still make you sorry, Nathan Lasco."

The grinding began again, the noise from the previous encounters. It filled the house to the rafters, a strange, metallic scraping.

"Shawn, is that you?" asked Carrie, her attention still on the machine.

*Beep beep.*

"Is it what you're warning us about?"

The loudest beep yet—long and insistent. Gunther looked at Helter, dropping the camera again. "Turn it off, man. This is too much, you have to turn it the fuck *off*."

"Turn what off?" asked Aury, swinging her narrowed gaze to Helter. When the kid didn't answer immediately, she pushed out of her chair and approached him, shouting to be heard over the grinding. "What's he talking about, Helter? What the fuck have you done?"

Helter put his hands up but drew closer to her, a dumb move if Nate ever saw one. Aury was almost incandescent. "Nothing out of the ordinary, I promise. This is all standard investigation stuff. That's why you hired us, right?"

Stella lifted her head slowly. "Hired you?" she asked, eyes wide.

Gunther slapped a hand over his eyes and groaned while Helter tried to backpedal. "No, I misspoke, not hired, just, uh, signed on with us."

Nate could almost see Stella's rage rise through her, lips tightening, her body shaking. "You conniving little bitch," she hissed.

Aury didn't so much as look at her, keeping her focus on Helter. "Tell me what you did. What does Gunther want you to turn off?"

"Ionizers," said Nate. "Air purifiers—they're in every room. They're meant to—"

She sliced her hand through the air and he shut up. "I know what the fuck they're for, and you were *not* supposed to use any shit like that. Monitoring only, didn't we agree on that?"

Helter stepped closer still and Nate decided the kid must have a death wish. At least, until he reached for Aury's hand. The little shit *did* have a crush. Or were they involved? Nate's heart lifted unexpectedly. Maybe Aury did have a chance at happiness.

Nate cleared his throat, intervened to save Helter from annihilation. "Hey, it's okay, I turned them off before we started. Carrie found them, and we didn't want anything to enhance . . . whatever the hell this is."

Aury jerked out of Helter's grip, loathing curling her lips. "This house does *not* need any fucking help. Do you have any idea what you've done?"

Katy trembled violently beside Nate and he tried to placate one sister and calm the other. "Did you hear me? We turned them off before this started. No harm, no foul, right?"

Aury's fiery gaze was only for Helter. "Is that true? Is that how it works? Turn it off and everything goes back to normal? Or is there residual effect?"

Helter opened and closed his mouth, his eyes wide.

Gunther pushed to his feet. "Tell her, man, or I will."

Carrie rose and moved next to Aury. "Tell her what? What else is there? Another machine?"

Helter dropped his head, unable to hold Aury's gaze any longer. "It was only to help. I swear, that's the only reason."

Aury stepped closer, toe to toe with the kid and he didn't take a step back. "What. Is it."

"Look, we started out by the book. No enhancing anything, just straight talking. But when stuff started happening last time, and then came to a halt all of a sudden, I figured we needed a little help. So, yeah, we added the ionizers. They're pretty low impact anyway, more of a little boost."

"But?" prompted Carrie.

"But . . . there's something else. Not an ionizer. On the third floor."

Carrie met Nate's gaze, her own wide. "Did you?" she asked.

"No, I . . . I didn't go up there." And he didn't want to, now, but if Carrie asked him, he would.

Mark stood. "I'll go. I've got it. Where is the thing? What's it look like?"

Nate felt a wash of real gratitude, his tension easing.

"It's a Jacob's Ladder," said Gunther, his jaw muscles bunching.

"You crass fucking fool," Aury almost whispered.

"What the fuck is a Jacob's Ladder?" asked Nate when no one bothered to explain. "What does it do?"

"It's another tool used to summon, but it uses electricity. A lot of it. There's a transformer, and it sends high voltages up between two rods. It arcs between them until it gets released at the top, and puts out a shit ton of electrons." Gunther's big hands moved as he spoke, describing the motion of the machine.

"And what does that do?" asked Katy in a trembling voice.

Helter swallowed. "It . . . theoretically, it provides energy to spirits. They can use it to manifest more fully, have more influence on the environment as long as it's on. It's probably how Shawn's been able to use the box." He fixed a pleading look on Aury. "So it's a good thing, right?"

"Oh, fuck," whispered Nate, looking at Gunther. "Last time, you said . . . you told him to turn it off, but I thought you meant a projector or something. A fake."

Helter shook his head. "No, I told you before, we don't do that. No fakes. What happened then, and what's happening now, it's *real*."

Aury's eyes narrowed. "Has it been running this whole time? Since the last time we tried this?"

"No, no way. I told you, we started off with nothing."

"Then what the fuck did Gunther want you to turn off yesterday?"

Helter shuffled his feet. "Okay, yeah, we used it briefly. Low voltage, barely running, and I turned it off after Stella's accident. Today's the first time we've used it for real."

Nate's jaw dropped. "*Ever?* So you decided to what, use us as your guinea pigs, without knowing what it could do?"

Aury turned her back on Helter and addressed herself to Gunther. "Turn it off. Now."

Mark strode toward the stairs. "Fuck it, we don't need their permission. I'll turn it off."

"No!" shouted Gunther with force, at the same time two beeps sounded from the talk box. Mark stopped and stared.

"Look, you can't just go up there and mess with it," Gunther said, calmer this time. "The voltage on that thing is high as fuck. Like, over 500 volts high. You touch that shit in the wrong spot and you'll fry."

"Jesus," exploded Nate. "You guys set a fucking death trap up there and didn't say shit about it? Are you trying to kill us?"

"Never," said Helter in a low voice, approaching Aury again. "I'm trying to help you. All of you. You wanted this to work. You wanted to know what happened, and you told me how many times you'd been let down in the past. That she'd promise, get you worked up, then pull the football at the last second. I wanted to make sure that didn't happen again, so yeah, I gave the house a little boost." He reached out to touch her arm and she knocked his hand away, but he pressed on. "I wanted you to know, once and for all, what killed your brother."

Nate's eyes widened and he turned to the talk box. "Fuck it, we have our witness right here. Shawn, you still around?"

*Beep.*

"Did Stella do it? Is she the one who killed you?"

Stella lunged to her feet shrieking, her hands extended, fingers curled into claws as she launched herself at Nate. Shawn was too quick for her.

*Beep. Beep beep.*

They all froze, staring at the box, the only sound the gradually rising grind that set Nate's teeth vibrating, and Stella's labored breathing.

"What's that mean?" asked Nate, the tension in his body bringing a wave of aches upon him. "Yes, or no?"

*Beep. Beep beep.*

"Yes *and* no?" asked Carrie.

*Beep.*

Confusion was etched on every countenance.

"How can that—" began Katy, but before she could finish her sentence Stella surged to the center of the circle, took the blinking talk box in both hands and threw it to the floor as hard as she could.

The box crunched when it hit, splinters of plastic flying in all directions. One shard caught Nate's cheek but he didn't feel the cut, or the trickle of warm blood that flowed from it. His attention was all on the box, broken beyond repair. He watched the blinking lights fade, then die, one by one.

It felt like grief. Like losing Shawn all over again. Failing him again. Fucking it up while his brother's eyes drained of life, at the hands of Stella once more while Nate stood by, unable to make himself move.

Nate's gaze rose slowly to the murderer. His vision flipped like lenses at the eye doctor—*which one's clearer? This, or this?*

Nate thought he'd never seen so clear in all his life. Everything was in sharp focus, the colors and depths cleaner than they'd ever been. He felt a sweeping rage, the increased heart rate, the burn of adrenaline coursing through him, but he didn't feel out of control. He felt great, in fact, in just the right mindset to finish this.

"You fucking cunt," he said, taking a step toward her.

All at once the breeze rose again, Helter's remaining equipment going nuts. The candles snuffed out, not in a single gust but one at a time, each emitting a crackle as its flame died. Whatever was doing it moved fast, heading in a line straight toward Stella, until only one remained lit, just behind where she stood. The darkness gathered close around her, a single flickering spotlight setting her at center stage, where she'd always wanted to be. Her eyes were wide but Nate couldn't tell if she'd even seen what happened, her mask of humanity nowhere in sight. His heart hammered, his palms sweating as he held tight to his sisters' hands, but they held onto each other all the harder.

"What the fuck?" breathed Helter from behind the camera he'd picked up once Gunther set it down. "What is it? What did that?"

Stella froze in place, her body stiff, eyes forward. Her breaths came fast and shallow, hands shaking at her sides. This time Mark kept his distance, but Nate could hardly blame him. His attention was caught by the sense of something looming just behind Stella's chair. There was a different quality to the darkness, a heaviness, impenetrable. His own breathing became erratic as memories crashed into him from somewhere buried deep.

He'd seen that kind of darkness before, those shadows, and not just in his dreams. Here, in this house, and maybe after, he couldn't be sure. He remembered waking one night from a terrible nightmare and sensing something hovering just above him. As his eyes adjusted, he'd seen a thicker shadow in the outline of a woman. With his own breath held, he heard *it* breathe, in and out in low, even breaths. Then it cocked its head in a sudden movement and Nate exploded out of his bed, screaming, running through the shadow creature in his desperation to get out of the room.

Had he told anyone about it? Was it even a real memory, or one planted or suggested by Stella's bullshit? He wished he knew, but either way, the shadow was here, now, looming over his mother. He looked at Carrie—could she see it, too?

"You lined us up," said Aury, her tone as dead and lifeless as ever. At some point she'd turned her back on Helter, her attention returned to the task at hand. "All four of us together, in front of that door."

Katy's chest hitched and Nate ground his teeth against the assault of memory. He wanted to stop Aury so he didn't have to feel it, so he could shove it down deep and look away, the way he'd been doing ever since that day. But then it would all be for nothing, and he couldn't bear that. So he took a breath and let himself feel everything. The overwhelming, impotent anger of a teenage boy in the face of a greater force. The trembling fear—they'd been here before, many times, but this time felt different. This time there was hope, too, even if he couldn't understand it.

"Yes," Stella said, sounding almost robotic. "I needed you all to see, to understand. You didn't know what kind of danger you were in, every time you hurt me."

Mark groaned softly and put his face in his hands, and

Nate felt a fierce flash of satisfaction. *Feel bad, fucker. This is what you left us to.*

"You meant to kill Shawn that night," said Aury. "You planned to from the start."

Stella swayed in place, not answering. Nate moved to Aury's side and took her hand, pulling Katy behind him. He wouldn't let his sister face this alone.

"You brought the bat with you. You knew you were going to do it. To hit him between the eyes."

"I hit him," Stella repeated, but still Nate couldn't tell if it was a confession, or mindless mimicry.

"You hit him," said Carrie.

"Yes."

"And when the children were all lined up, all giving you their full attention, and Shawn was incapacitated—what happened then?"

A burst of sulfuric stench hit Nate just as twin blue flames sparked in the darkness behind Stella. The thing leaned over her, those dead blue lights hanging just over her head. Its outline wavered, shrunk. Became something familiar.

Stella lifted her chin, grinned at Carrie, her own eyes burning blue. "What happened next? They learned their lesson, of course."

The shadow that now bore her shape lunged forward and consumed her, its ephemeral form swallowing her whole until the two monsters merged. For the space of a breath, no one moved, all eyes on Stella. A breath was the only reprieve they had. As the last candle went out, Stella shot from her chair and wrapped herself around Helter, knocking them both to the ground, her nails gouging the soft flesh of his jaws. Her teeth clacked together swiftly, an inhuman, rapid-fire *thocking* issuing from her mouth, coming for Helter at high speed as Stella lowered her face toward his eyes. He had time for a single scream of raw terror before the light went out, his cries subsumed by wet, meaty tearing.

# CHAPTER TWENTY-ONE

"**N**o!" **SCREAMED KATY,** pulling herself from Nate's clutch and running for Helter. Gunther cried out but Nate could see nothing of the melee in the midst of the broken circle.

"Katy!" Nate called, his panic rising. "Katy come back, get away from her!"

Those teeth still gnashed in the darkness, the clack of their meeting now muffled by a layer of flesh. Nate had no way of knowing who Stella had in her grip. Had she finished Helter and moved on to her youngest daughter? He tried to move forward but Aury's hand in his pulled him up short.

"Don't go in blind—that's what she wants. Don't let her finish the job she started with Shawn. I can't lose all of you," Aury said on a sob.

Nate hesitated, squinting in the darkness, looking for a way through to Katy. The blackness was absolute, unbroken in a way that wasn't natural. No street or moonlight penetrated the hell the Lascos had descended to, but Nate didn't have time to worry about it. He held tight to Aury's hand and leaned close.

"Never again. I'll never let us be separated again."

Loud crashes and screams filled the air, that nauseating stench of sulfur growing worse. Above it all came the scraping, grinding sound coming from the third floor. It was maddeningly familiar. The memory it tapped was on the edge of his consciousness, but Nate couldn't push it into the light. He told himself it didn't matter, not right now. Instead he tried to orient himself, hindered by the insanity around him. It felt like dozens of bodies moving in the dark, blocking his path to Katy, slamming into his shoulder from the front, his leg from the back. It was a mosh pit from hell, stirred into a frenzy by a steady flow of negative energy. Then the darkness was broken by strobing slivers of white light, revealing the scene in stop-motion flashes that were somehow so much worse than the blindness of pitch black. There were faces everywhere, but none of them were Katy's. Helter ran past screaming, and for a moment relief flooded Nate. Stella hadn't killed the kid, so maybe it wasn't as bad as it sounded.

Then Helter's hands dropped from his face as his unseeing eyes met Nate's. Nate gagged. Chunks of flesh were missing from both sides of his jawline, bleeding furrows torn down his eyes and cheeks. One eye drooped low, dangling from its socket. Nate couldn't tell in the uncertain strobing light, but he thought the eye looked deflated, drained of fluid. He took a step forward, reaching for Helter, but a gargling scream surged from the other man's throat and he disappeared behind a heaving wall of bodies.

When Nate tried to follow, Aury again pulled him back.

"Katy's the priority," she said harshly.

As shitty as he felt about abandoning Helter to his fate, Nate knew she was right. He turned away with effort, searching every passing visage for his sister. He recognized none of them, and his flesh went cold, wondering how many lost souls wandered among them. Men, women— and, in some cases, children—there in one flash, gone in the next. That made no sense—no fucking sense at all. It had to be a hallucination of some kind. Disoriented and approaching panic, unable to push through the scrum, he leaned close to Aury to be heard over the swell of anguished voices.

"Who the fuck are these people?"

Aury's voice was stony. "I don't give a shit. They're not Katy. Focus, Nate—what do we do?"

Nate's thoughts were scattershot but he tried to reel them in, concentrate. Losing the light shouldn't have fucked everything up so bad, but it was more than that. The thing, the ghost or demon or whatever, it was real, and it had taken Stella over. The others now crowding the room must have something to do with that, as though the gates of hell had opened, spilling the tormented through the second floor.

"Katy," he bellowed as loud as he could. "Katy, get away from her and come back to us. Where the fuck are you?"

"Let me get my phone," said Aury in his ear, and let go of his hand for seconds only. It felt like a lifetime that his hand was empty and he floated, unmoored in the dark. Then she took his hand again and cursed. "It's not working—I don't understand. I can't get the flashlight to turn on, or the screen to light up at all."

Nate tried his with the same result, his panic growing when Katy screamed from somewhere far to his right, a wheezing note to it. His body went cold—the staircase.

"Katy, stop! Stand right where you are, don't take another step! We'll come get you."

Her only answer was another scream, thinner and more desperate than the last, and the thud of bodies on wood. He waited for the tumble, the sickening crack of bone, but instead the sounds moved up and away.

Stella was taking her to the third floor.

### ★★★

A cool hand brushed his face and Nate flinched, then sagged when he recognized Carrie's scent. He squinted and made out her face in the brief strobes of light.

"Nate? Are you okay?"

"It's Katy—I have to find her. She screamed, and I think she's having an asthma attack. Then I heard, on the steps—"

"I know. Is Aury with you?" she asked, squinting over his shoulder.

"Yes," he said, clutching his sister's hand.

"Good. Don't let go of each other—remember, you've always had strength in numbers. Where's everyone else?"

"I don't—the only one I saw was Helter." Nausea surged again as the image of the kid's ruined face filled his mind. "He's hurt bad."

"Okay. I'll go back for him—you've got to find your sister. Come with me."

Her hand clasped his free one and she tugged him forward.

She guided them through the chaos to the base of the stairs, put Nate's hand on the banister. "Go slow," she said close to his ear. "You don't know what's up there."

He looked up, his gaze stopping at each stair. Eleven of them, and why the hell was that? It should be thirteen, something ominous, something to explain the hell this house harbored. When his eyes reached the top, his breath froze in his chest. The creature with the white shirt stood there unmoving, staring down.

Nate's hands shook, his voice unsteady. "Katy?" he called as loud as he could. She didn't answer, but above the fray was the sound of ripping tape, and the creak of a door.

The creature—no, not a creature, his brother. Shawn. He moved at last, lifting one bony hand from his side, opening it to beckon Nate up. Up those eleven stairs he'd seen in his nightmares more times than he could count, always waking before he reached the top and saw what he needed to see. Nate couldn't breathe as hope and terror fought for dominance.

Aury gave no sign of seeing the apparition, and when Nate looked again, it was gone.

"She's taking her in there," Aury cried, shoving past him as the metal grinding sound followed, clearer than ever and getting closer. Aury's eyes went wide, teeth gritted. "The bat. That's what the sound is. She brought it in with them that night, do you remember?"

He did, with sudden clarity. He'd blocked that detail out with so many others, but the cold in his chest wouldn't let him escape the connotations. Stella had dragged the bat behind her, a slow, metallic grinding, the same as what reverberated throughout the house. She'd brought the bat behind closed doors because she meant to use it, just as she'd meant to when she first wielded it. The blow to Shawn's head hadn't been enough—she'd meant to finish him off. And had she planned to stop with him, or were all of them on the chopping block that day? It was all too likely—Stella, planning to take them all out, only prevented by Shawn's sacrifice.

And now she had Katy.

"Not again," said Nate between clenched teeth, and followed his sister at top speed, stumbling twice and barking his shins on the steps. The second time, he looked down and realized he could see the stair, and not just in brief flashes. He bent, catching sight of a small white tube with an orange cap: Katy's inhaler. He grabbed it, shoved it in his pocket. When he glanced up again there was a dim glow around the edges of the door. "Fuck," he breathed.

"I see it," said Aury, as he reached the top step beside her.

They were in time to see Stella's face, framed by that low red light, her eyes empty, lips curled in a cruel grin, a horrifying replica of how she'd looked the day Shawn died. Then she slammed the door in their faces, and Katy screamed.

"No!" Nate lunged at the door, his shoes sliding in the inch-thick dust, falling hard on his right side and smashing his face into the wood.

Aury reached for him in the gloom, the third floor still lit by the eerie glow of the door, seeping from the edges. She pulled Nate to his feet and went to it, yanking the knob, throwing her shoulder into it when the lock didn't give. It didn't so much as move in its frame, and she cast him a look of panic. He went to her side, wiping the sweat from his palms on his jeans. He forced himself to slow down, to move with intent. *When you rush you fuck it up. Don't fuck this up.*

Hands shaking, he closed his eyes and tried the knob. It stuck fast, no movement to either side. Following Aury's example he threw his shoulder into the thick wood, jarring it to the socket, knocking the breath from his chest.

"Fuck," he growled after several fruitless attempts. Breathing hard, his ire rising by the second. "Was this part of your plan?" He hadn't meant it to sound so accusatorial, but there it was, out in the open.

Tears squeezed from the corners of her eyes, and she looked wild, less in control than he'd ever seen. "None of this was part of my plan. I didn't think it would get this bad, and I never approved Helter using any of this shit. Do you really think I'd hurt Katy? Hurt you?"

*You've been hurting us this whole time.* He managed to bite back the words. He understood her compulsion, her need to do something to strike back against Stella, but all of this had been a mistake. He could see in her face she knew that at least as well as he did and his anger died.

"It's my fault. I get that, okay?" she said in a desperate undertone. "Let me make this right, get Katy safe, then you can berate me all you want."

He frowned. "I wasn't—"

Aury turned away, hammered on the door with both fists. "Let us in! Let us in, you fucking bitch!" she screamed. There was no reply. The grinding sound had stopped, the house eerily silent. The feel of rising energy made the air heavy, Nate's fillings aching, a migraine spiking behind his eyes.

Tears ran down Aury's face, eyes wild and her mouth half-open. "What do we do? We can't leave them in there together."

Nate nodded, breathing hard, and stood shoulder to

shoulder with his sister. A sense of deja vu crashed over him, but it was no mental glitch. They'd been here before, in this exact place. The day of the door had come round again. He looked to his other side, half expecting Shawn to be standing there, fists clenched, going hell for leather to get their youngest member back. Nate would have welcomed him in whatever form he took, no matter how horrifying.

But Shawn wasn't beside them. Hadn't been for a long time, no matter what Nate believed about what he'd seen and heard in this house. He could accept the idea of Shawn communicating, of him appearing as either a warning or a guide, but Shawn couldn't save them this time. He couldn't stand between the rest of them and Stella anymore, and that was Nate's fault, too. He'd let it happen. But what the fuck could he have done? What could he do now?

*Strength in numbers.* Carrie always came back to that, and it felt like the truth. But their numbers were smaller than ever, only two of them left facing off against the door, and Nate had so little to offer. Always frozen with indecision, anything he did was too little, too late.

*So give in to it. Do what you were made to do, and make her hurt like she hurt Shawn.*

Nate felt like a bucket of cold water had been thrown over him, the panic doused by intense terror. The grinding voice from his dreams, the one that delighted in hurting people—it came from inside his head. A manifestation of his own subconscious, surely. No other explanation made sense, but why did it feel so . . . other? Was it Shawn? It didn't sound like him, or feel like him. Was it separate, then? Or was it the dark thing Shawn was afraid of, the part that made him fear who he was, and what he might do? Had there really been something inside his brother, the same as Stella?

*Only his anger. You have it, too—you're capable of just as much violence as him. As Stella. Stop fighting it and give in.*

Nate stood frozen, afraid to move, to think, as though the voice inside his head would see his desire to hurt, to punish, and take that as consent. But that was ridiculous—the only voice in his head was his own. He wasn't possessed, he was just a fucked-up human, with the violent tendencies he'd inherited. Carrie was right. He'd always fought them, kept them under strict control, but what if that was the wrong approach? Would giving in to that nature, releasing the beast coiled inside his DNA, would that give them the upper hand they needed? Was that what Shawn had done the day he died? Nate hoped so. Whatever really happened behind that door, he hoped his brother hadn't held back.

A voice from the stairs broke the spell. "Aury? Nate?"

It was Gunther, breathing hard, blood dripping from a cut over one eye. He stared at them, then saw the door. "Is she in there?"

"Yes," sobbed Aury.

Gunther shouted down the stairs. "Ms. Barker? Helter? Mark? We need help, get up here, now."

Seconds later Carrie scurried up the steps, her hair a mess, one shoe missing. "I don't know where Mark is, but Helter's hurt. Stella did a number on him. There's a lot of blood, but he wouldn't let me close enough to look. He's able to breathe, at least."

She gestured to the door. "She still in there?"

"We couldn't . . . it won't . . . "

Gunther nodded and went to it, looking it over. Whatever concern he might have felt for Helter had been pushed down by the need to get to Katy.

"We already tried breaking it down," Nate said numbly. "It's too strong."

The big man sidestepped the door and went rummaging in the far corners of the third floor. Carrie held Nate's hand while they waited, all of them listening hard for what might be taking place on the other side of that door, but there was only that heavy silence.

"The Jacob's Ladder," said Carrie. "Did you turn it off?"

Nate looked around the wide, open loft. "I didn't see it."

Carrie frowned. "I don't either, but if there's even a chance something's drawing power from it . . . "

"Yeah," Nate agreed grimly. He took a few steps in each direction, searching the gloom for an arc of electricity. There was nothing.

"Gunther?" he called. It should have been too loud in the echoing space, but the air up here was thick, refusing to carry sound. "Gunther!"

He looked up, his face half in shadow, half lit by that damned red light. "What? What's happened?"

"Where's the Ladder?"

Gunther's eyes widened and he dropped what he was doing, went jogging to the east side of the room, cursing when he stumbled over some unseen obstacle. He squinted into the darkness before turning back to Nate, eyes wide. "It's gone."

"You mean it's turned off?" asked Carrie.

"No, I mean it's fucking *gone*. The machine's not there anymore, and neither is the transformer." He frowned. "But like, I still *feel* it. That kinda current in the air?"

Nate felt it too, but it didn't matter. Katy's time was running out. "Forget it, let's just get in there." He looked frantically around the room, then caught sight of the dull gleam of metal. For a moment, he felt a stomach-dropping certainty it was the bat, but when he pointed and Gunther picked up a long metal slat, he recognized it as a piece of an old bed frame.

Gunther grinned. "Fuck yeah. Let's see how this wooden piece of shit holds up to good old-fashioned iron."

Nate helped Gunther drag it to the door, trying not to hear the grinding, scraping sound it made against the hardwood. He closed his eyes against the image of an aluminum bat making contact with his little sister's face, then pushed it away. He owed her more than a coward's avoidance.

"Let's do it. Not in the middle, though—get it over by the jam. We're gonna pry this baby open."

Gunther nodded and they worked together, ramming the metal slat as hard as they could into the door facing by the latch. It took several tries and cut hands all around, but they managed to splinter the wood enough to get purchase. In the brief pause between hits, Stella's voice rang out. Nate couldn't understand anything she said, but she sounded unhinged, shrieking like a harpy. A choking noise followed and almost did him in.

Tears streamed down Aury's face. "It's Shawn all over again."

Nate had no words to comfort her—for the Lasco children, defeat felt inevitable. Their escape had always been temporary, their lives away from Stella a hollow stage show, less real with every passing minute.

"Fuck that noise," said Gunther. "Come help me push this thing—put your backs into it."

With all four of them pushing as hard as they could against the makeshift pry bar, it wasn't long before the wood gave and the door broke away, sagging slightly inward, the reddish glow from inside making everything look blood-soaked.

Aury held Nate's gaze, a conversation without words, the way close siblings do. They weren't close, not by a long shot, and maybe they never had been because of Stella's seeds of dissension. But they were the Lasco kids, and they banded together when the shit hit the fan.

Aury turned to Gunther and Carrie. "Stay out here, please. It has to be Nate and me."

Gunther held the metal slat like a bayonet. "You'll need us—you don't know what she might be capable of, with that thing inside her."

Nate took Aury's hand, wondering if she was thinking the same thing. That they didn't want witnesses for what they might be forced to do. "We know that better than anyone. Stay here in case we need you. Carrie, can you call 911? See if your phone works outside the house."

She didn't argue, hurrying down the stairs, and Gunther grudgingly stood aside, still hefting his weapon.

Brother and sister wasted no more time. They took a breath as one and shoved through, at long last facing what lay beyond the door.

# CHAPTER TWENTY-TWO

**N**ATE RUSHED INTO the room, Aury's hand in his, gritting his teeth at the volume of noise that greeted him. Whatever silence had hovered outside, chaos increased ten-fold within. The endless grinding scrape of the bat on the wood floor, the nauseating impact of metal on flesh, followed by a choking, wet gargle of tortured breath. Then the whole thing cycled over and started again, a loop from hell that seemed to come from everywhere at once.

The air felt heavier than ever and Nate's hair rose on end. He felt like his brain would start leaking from his ears and couldn't get oriented. Aury tugged his hand, pulling him to the far wall of the big room where the remainder of his truncated family were locked in battle. He couldn't see them at first—they knelt behind the desk that shouldn't still be there, the same one where Shawn lost his life, and when they came into sight it was a confusing mash of flailing limbs and hair. He let go of Aury, dropped to his knees next to Katy and took her shoulder, trying to pull her away.

"Let go, let the fuck go of her, I'm not letting you do this!" he screamed. He pulled with all his might and managed to get Katy free, fumbling in his pocket for her inhaler. "Here, take this. Katy, *breathe*, please."

"Let go of me, let go, let go," Katy shrieked, wheezing and struggling in his hold. "I won't let her do it again, I won't let her fucking win."

It took several seconds to realize Stella's hands were wrapped around her own throat, fighting to get breath through her bruised airway. She pushed herself away from her raging daughter, scrabbling on her ass until she ran into Aury, and with a sob threw herself at her oldest daughter's legs.

"She's crazy," she said, her own voice high and hysterical. "She's trying to kill me!"

Nate looked at Katy, still struggling against him, her teeth bared, saliva flying with every word she spat. Her airway sounded strained, but not closed off, and he let the inhaler fall to his side. There were no marks on her neck, no river of blood covering her face as he'd been sure he'd see. She had no visible injuries at all, and he tried to understand.

"*You* were choking *her*?" he asked, his grip loosening.

Katy seethed in a way that reminded him uncomfortably of Stella. "She's going to do it again. Take my family from me, send me back to be alone forever, just like her." Her eyes were bright not only with tears, but rage. "I didn't see it before, the way you guys did. I really thought we could fix it, make a family again. But she *wants* to ruin our lives, to make us hurt, and I won't let her do it. Not this time."

Aury frowned down at her sobbing mother. "What the hell is happening in here? Why the fuck did you drag her upstairs?"

Stella hid her face against Aury's knees. "That wasn't me—I didn't do it. The . . . the *thing*, it was here, inside me."

"That thing? You mean your *friend?*" Nate spat.

Stella shuddered. "Now it's inside *her*." She jerked her head at Katy. "Just like what happened with Shawn." She devolved further, incoherent above her sobs.

Nate looked at his youngest sister again, tried to get her to meet his eyes. Would he even know if she wasn't herself? Would he recognize twin blue flames where her sweet hazel gaze should be? The only difference he saw was in the determined set of her shoulders, the clench of her jaw. A doormat no more.

"What makes you think it's inside her?" Aury asked, still standing, arms crossed and ignoring Stella's clutch on her legs. Gone was the woman with tears on her face, panicking over her sister. She was aloof as ever, and Nate fought a sense of unease. He didn't have a handle on the situation, wanted to call time out and think it through.

Stella wailed even louder. "Didn't you *see* what she was doing? She was trying to kill me, and she wanted . . . she wanted to . . . oh, God." She dissolved into incoherence, but Nate's gaze followed the direction of her pointing finger.

His eyes widened when he recognized the knife laying off to the side, blade open and shining. Shawn's knife, the one he'd been buried with. The one that appeared their first day of filming, that Nate had carried ever since. He felt his pocket and found it empty.

"She was going to use it on me!" shrieked Stella, her face covered in mascara and snot. "She pinned my arm down, said she'd take the rest of my fingers."

"Why not?" asked Katy in a low growl, her breathing easier. "Wouldn't be the first time, would it? Just following in big brother's footsteps."

"Shawn never used his knife on her," said Aury, shouting to be heard above the high decibel grinding. "It never made any sense, that she'd just let him saw her damn fingers off."

"That's not true!" screamed Stella. "He used that knife on me, his own mother. And then he turned it on himself."

"Liar!" Katy lunged at her and Nate barely caught her in time. He held her numbly, frozen in place.

"You said it was an accident. That he fell, hit the desk just right."

Stella raised soulful eyes to his. "I did that for you kids. To spare you the truth of what your brother had become. But now you need to know. Shawn killed himself. Cut his own throat, right in front of me."

Nate's face went hot, then cold, sweat beading on his

upper lip, mouth going dry. The knife, and Stella's missing fingers had been a key point in the eventual determination of accidental death by the coroner. She'd appeared catatonic, unable to answer questions, though Nate figured it was an act. Someone had tossed out the idea of self-defense—after all, Shawn had been much bigger, and armed with a blade. An out-of-control adolescent—he had to be the one at fault. So what if she'd shoved him a little too hard? Stella's bleeding stumps, the horror of those missing appendages, swayed the detective in charge. Whatever else had happened behind that door, she'd clearly been afraid for her life.

Nate had seen his brother pocket the knife before the confrontation, when they'd heard the low fury in her voice as she called their names. He didn't have to ask his brother to know it was a weak measure of security, an attempt at self-defense that was more than deserved. The outside world didn't get that. They hadn't grown up on the ever-shifting ground of Stella's making, so they couldn't see a reason for Shawn to bring a knife into a closed room with his mother. Forget that she brought her own weapon, with every intent to use it.

"You sick *bitch*," he spat, voice trembling. "I never believed your lame ass accident story, and now you want us to think he fucking killed himself? Bullshit. *You* did that."

Katy raked her nails against his arm. "Let me the fuck go. I don't want to hear another word from her."

"The only prints they found on that knife were his," said Stella with eerie calm, her uncontrolled passion tucked away like she was shedding a costume. "Explain that to me, Nathan."

"That's a fucking lie."

"No, it's true," said Aury. "Shawn's were the only prints."

Nate turned on her, his jaw dropped. "How the fuck would you know that?"

Aury stepped forward. "I finally got them to open the file. And yes, the knife only had his prints."

Nate turned back to Stella. The smug pinch of her eyes, the sneer of her lips made his stomach churn. "I don't believe it," he said numbly, his confidence wavering. He lost his grip on Katy, but she'd stopped moving, staring at Stella and breathing hard.

Stella tossed her hair. "It's true. But you mustn't blame your brother. He wasn't in control, any more than I was when my friend was inside me. He did it all, then he turned the knife on himself."

"Even if I believe the shit about the fingerprints, I *don't* believe that."

"True again," Aury said. "The knife wound on his neck—the autopsy determined it was self-inflicted."

Stella's nostrils flared as she turned on Aury. "Autopsy? I never agreed to that."

Aury laughed. "Oh, I know that. I don't have any idea why the authorities acquiesced, or if they even did. I didn't find record of an initial autopsy. But *I* commissioned one, and the findings are solid. I paid for the best. Shawn cut his own throat."

Nate felt the ground shift once more. What the hell was this? Why was Aury defending Stella?

"Why would he do that?" he asked in a small voice.

Stella lifted her chin. "I told you. It was the entity. It had hold of him. No one could be blamed for what they did under its influence."

Nate saw the trap she'd set for them too late. To continue believing in his brother, he'd have to forgive his mother. Or at least that was how she saw it, but there were worlds of difference between their actions. He shook his head. "He didn't fucking kill himself."

"You're right," said Aury. "He didn't."

Katy's face was nearly expressionless. "I don't understand. You said—"

"I said the knife wound was self-inflicted. I didn't say that's what killed him."

Nate straightened. "Then what did?"

Aury bent and retrieved something from behind the standing bookshelf. "This," she said, brandishing the aluminum bat that lived in their nightmares. She stepped closer to Stella.

Nate's gaze was pulled inexorably to the bat, following every tiny movement. "That can't be the same one."

"No?" She shrugged. "Does it matter?"

He couldn't tear his gaze from it. "How did it get in here? This place has been locked."

"And who has the key?" she asked.

He looked at Stella but she was laser focused on Aury. "I'm warning you," she hissed, but Aury kept advancing, stopping only when her mother was in range of the bat.

"He was hit a few places—the head, like we saw." She tapped Stella lightly with the end of the bat right where the blow had fallen on Shawn.

Stella flinched away but didn't otherwise move.

"A pretty solid knock here," Aury continued, touching the side of the bat to Stella's right hip. "Fractured a little shard of bone off. And then here." She tapped Stella's left shoulder, the tension building with each contact. "Here," she said softly, brushing the bat against her mother's jaw with a tenderness Stella certainly hadn't bothered with.

Nate closed his eyes against a rush of tears, remembering the sounds from behind the door that day. The meaty thud of blows landing, bone cracking. He pictured Shawn taking each hit with his teeth bared, his anger growing.

"But the real problem, the one that got him, was here." Aury moved closer still and extended the bat so the end rested against Stella's throat. "Enough force to crush his windpipe, to the point he couldn't get any air at all." She lowered her chin. "He never hit the desk. It was you."

Nate realized the noises had stopped. The dragging, the smack of metal on flesh, and the wet, gargling wheeze. Maybe there was no need to remind them, now that they knew what it meant. It was Shawn, desperate for air as his oxygen-starved brain went into panic mode. Hot tears slid down Nate's cheeks, stinging the cut there. Katy bent her head and gave in to sobs.

"He suffered," she choked out. "You made him suffer, so much."

Stella's gaze darted between her children. She licked her lips. "He did it to himself. He . . . he took it from me. I've always said that—he got it away from me, I was injured, my hand was pouring blood, and he—"

Aury's voice cut through Stella's words. "Before you spin another lie, you might be interested to know they fingerprinted the bat, too. And yours were the only ones on it." She leaned in close. "All ten of them."

# CHAPTER TWENTY-THREE

**N**ATE'S BODY TURNED to stone. His blood frozen in his veins, his heart refusing to beat as his flailing brain made sense of what Aury said. Ten fingerprints meant Stella killed Shawn first, then sawed off her own fingers to remove suspicion. He wanted to puke.

"But . . . " stuttered Katy. "You said the knife, it only had Shawn's prints. What happened to her fingers?"

Aury shrugged. "I'm assuming that was after the fact, when she had the leisure to do it. The prints were smeared, covered in blood. I'm betting she put her hands over his to make it look like he held the knife."

Nate choked, turned on Stella. "You used his *body*, his dead body to incriminate him after you beat him to death? After he suffocated because you crushed his airway?"

Stella didn't respond save the movement of her blank, too-wide eyes, but Aury nodded. "That's why he used the knife on himself, right before he died. Because he couldn't breathe."

"What?" asked Nate, frowning. "Why would—"

Aury smiled. "I expect it was all he could think to do. He wasn't trying to speed his death, before you make that accusation," said Aury, whipping her head around to Stella once more, steel in her voice. She pressed the bat harder into Stella's throat, eliciting a soft choking cough.

"Then what?" asked Nate.

Aury smiled again but kept her eye on Stella. "You remember watching *Anaconda*?"

Nate's brows came together. "Only about a hundred times. What the hell does that have to do with anything?"

"It wasn't just that movie—it was a popular trope back then. The emergency tracheotomy thing. TV made it look like all you needed was a pen and a sharp knife."

Katy moaned and Nate bit his lip, his stomach doing an unhappy flip. He thought of Shawn's panic, of his bravery in attempting something like that. What it must have taken for a seventeen-year-old kid to put a knife to his own throat, digging desperately in his flesh for a way to breathe.

"But it . . . didn't work," guessed Nate, his throat dry.

"Of course it didn't," Aury said softly. "He was a teenage boy, not an ER doctor. Damn if I'm not proud as hell of him for trying, though."

"I don't understand," said Katy. "If you knew all of this—if you found it out by commissioning an exhumation, the autopsy—then why are we here?" She gestured around the dimly-lit room, a picture of frozen chaos that might resume at any second. Waiting only for the right cue. "What was the point in all this?"

Aury shrugged. "I didn't start this rodeo. She did. At first I tried to talk her out of it—the last thing any of us needed was another excruciating build-up only to get sand kicked in our faces again." She knelt to get eye to eye with Stella. "But when she wouldn't let it go, I decided to take control. No more broken promises. No more bullshit." She lifted her lip, hatred sparking from her eyes. "I need to hear her say it. They're never going to reopen the case—I've tried, more than once. So I need her to take responsibility for what she did to Shawn—to all of us. And no amount of medical reports or other evidence, or God forbid, a fucking *conscience* is going to make her confess. Is it, Mommy dearest?"

Stella faced Nate, chin wobbling, bottom lip stuck out. She looked like she would protest, deny everything. Like she'd beseech his help. But he'd never been able to predict her. All at once her expression changed, her tears drying, the crumpled mouth turning upward in a sly smile. She raised one eyebrow and he knew, from years of seeing that swift, sickening change, she was about to do something she hoped would wreck his world.

She pushed to her feet and Aury let her, backing off with the bat. Stella straightened and tilted her head back. "He *was* the violent one. He intimidated me whenever he could, thought that just because he got taller than me, he could threaten me. He was violent. Out of control. I tried so hard to love him anyway, to look past what he was, but that day he crossed a line. That's why my friend came to help me."

Nate's hands trembled at his side. "You keep talking about this *friend*. What happened to all that scary shadow shit, the 'dark presence' and all that? You claimed something possessed you, made you do terrible things, but suddenly it's a friend?"

Her smile grew and she crossed her arms. "Yes, my *friend*. She took care of me when no one else would." The smile dropped and she narrowed her eyes, intent on her mission of destruction. "But I wasn't the only one possessed, Nathan." She spat his name, her body thrumming with fury. "When your brother dragged me in here, I saw that light in his eyes, and I *knew*—"

Katy screamed, and this time Nate made no move to hold her back. She stood panting, only a foot away from her cowering mother, and shoved a finger in her face.

"Don't you say it, don't you fucking accuse him!"

Stella didn't hesitate to finish firing her shot. "It was Shawn who was possessed with the bad thing. With the *real* evil in this house. He tried to kill me, but my friend was too fast for him."

Katy let out a cry and launched herself at her mother, but Aury pulled her aside, almost throwing her sister to the far side of the room. She turned to Stella, seething. "No more lies!"

"I'm the only reason he fought it as long as he did," Stella said. "If I hadn't been hard on him, if I hadn't kept on him every second of every day, he'd have let it in long before, and you'd all be dead, at *his* hand."

Nate gritted his teeth, clapped his hands to his ears like he could stop her words, shove them back by physical force. He was angrier than he could ever remember being, a crazy rage that felt like it would consume him.

*Not if you give in to it. Let go, and your fury will consume her, instead.*

Nate's shoulders sagged, his chest tight, stomach queasy. He couldn't remember the last time he'd had a good night's sleep, and all at once it caught up with him. His eyes burned, vision blurred around the edges. The voice was right—he was bone-tired. The long-term emotional exhaustion of holding himself together, keeping himself tightly wound enough that nothing could creep in without his knowledge, nothing else could get a finger hold on who he was or what he might do. Constant vigilance, and for what? A cold and empty life, and not enough strength to save his sisters? He remembered the dreams, those vivid, paralyzing dreams, and for the first time he pushed aside the horror of losing control, and welcomed the relief of letting go.

A single, wavering exhale of glorious defeat was followed immediately by a wash of ungovernable rage crashing over him, the kind that filled his belly with fire, sent explosive energy through his veins. He felt powerful, like he could pop his mother's head off, tear her lower jaw away, dig with his bare hands into the meat of her belly and pull her vital organs out one by one. He could make her suffer and bleed and squeal before he ended her reign of terror. All he had to do was follow the advice of every bullshit 90's movie and after school special: be himself. Be the rage filled, violent bastard he'd been born to be.

Before he could take a step, a cold, dry grip landed on his wrist.

His gaze dropped to the shriveled, dead hand that held his, and time stood still.

It wore the same white t-shirt it had in each visitation, the left sleeve rucked up higher than the right, revealing mottled flesh that faded into the darkness beyond. Above the stretched-out crew neck hung folds of loose, rotting flesh, blending into the chin of the thing, rising until taken over by a too-wide void of an open mouth. It hung open, displaying unnaturally long teeth, and above it, an upper lip shrunk back to where its nose would be, if it had one. And atop it all, fading into unknowable blackness, those empty, nothing eyes staring straight at him.

The seconds stretched endlessly as he held the gaze of the void, his flesh freezing, mouth dry. It was real. Shawn was real, and Nate no longer had the luxury of consigning him to the realms of imagination or suggestion. Shawn was here, with them, and Nate wondered if he always had been.

A low moan broke from Aury and she appeared at his shoulder, reaching for his free hand. "Shawn," she said in a voice devoid of hope. A tone that spoke of a lifetime of misery without expectation of relief.

Katy stood and came slowly to Nate's side, her frenzied anger doused the same as his had been. Nate let out a shaky sigh of relief. His sister had been no more possessed than he was; only justifiably enraged. She peered into the darkness. "That can't be him," she said in a shaking voice. "It's not Shawn."

When no one answered, her voice rose to a note of hysteria. "Aury. It's not him—that can't be him, he's, it's—"

Aury gestured to the thing in the shadows. "You forget, I've seen the autopsy photos, after he was exhumed."

Katy moaned. "Oh, Jesus. Shawn."

Nate spoke softly. "It's . . . it's okay, though." He turned back to the creature who still held his wrist. His eyes traveled up the white shirt to the dead visage of his brother, those nothing eyes fixed on him. Yet there *was* something there, even if it was hard to see. There was peace, and it spread to Nate, calming the fire in his veins, dulling the fear of what he saw. "It's really okay," he breathed again, and this time he knew it was true.

Haltingly, Aury drew closer. "Shawn," she said again.

"How?" asked Katy hollowly.

Nate saw it then, the burning blue arc in the darkness, rising between two clear plastic tubes somewhere in the shadows behind his brother. Not the flame of a devil's eyes, but the gleam of electricity. Jacob's Ladder, biblically a path between heaven and earth. Here in this room, that path was made by a spark of power, and for once, it belonged to them.

"No," Stella said in throbbing accents. Forgotten in the presence of her eldest son, she recalled their attention quickly as she moved with frightening speed. "*You're dead*," she shrieked.

"Stella," came a warning voice from the door. Mark stood there, framed in that place that delineated the before and after in the lives of all the Lascos. Nate blinked, having forgotten there was a world outside this room, one that wasn't governed by Stella and the things she drove them to.

"Put it down," Mark said heavily.

Nate whipped his gaze back and saw that Stella had somehow retrieved the bat, was wielding it with a snarl. He braced for her attack, to feel the slam of metal in vital places. He moved to stand between her and his sisters, his fists clenched.

But she wasn't coming for them. Nate frowned, trying to understand. What was she planning?

Sparking blue light reflected in her eyes and his stomach dropped. She was going for the Ladder.

"No!" he shouted, despair washing over him. He wouldn't make it in time, and Stella would once more sever the tenuous connection with their lost brother.

Aury snarled and lunged past him, Shawn's knife clutched in one hand, but it was Mark who got there first.

He grabbed Stella's shoulders, halting her progress, his gaze tender where he looked down at her. Nate thought Mark meant to kiss her, and he guessed by the way she lifted her face and parted her lips, that was her impression, too. But instead Mark swung her to the side, pushed her close to the arc of power from the Ladder. Let go of her just as the aluminum bat she held made contact with 500 volts.

# CHAPTER TWENTY-FOUR

**W**HEN HE WAS TEN, Nate had been electrocuted when he'd unplugged a cord from an old power strip. The current was weak, the shock lasting less than a second, but that wasn't how it felt. It was a burning pain in his fingers that held him in place as it ran up his arm, forced a scream from him even as he failed to make his limbs obey.

What coursed through Stella in the few seconds she was held upright was more than three times as much voltage, and there was no safety cutoff, nothing to stem the flow of arcing death. Nate held his breath as he watched her vibrate in place, her blue eyes wide, her mouth set in a rictus of pain. Her skin began to smoke, the hand that held the bat blackening, the skin peeling back in charred curls. Her hair stood on end and he had to stifle a crazy urge to laugh—she looked like a Saturday morning cartoon, a coyote getting his finger stuck in an Acme socket. But he didn't laugh, and he didn't look away, instead bearing witness to the end of his tormentor.

The light in the room flashed but he couldn't have said whether it was a response to the voltage, the flickering of the Jacob's Ladder, or something else entirely. When his gaze traveled past Stella to the darkness beyond, he saw Shawn standing there. It seemed with each flash of light Shawn's edges softened, his mottled flesh lightening, then smoothing out. The dead boy watched Stella's death from the other side, and if he felt joy or vindication, Nate couldn't tell. His last sight of his older brother was of the young man he'd been, restoring Nate's memories of him the way he should be. He didn't smile, nor make a gesture, but Nate understood his goodbye all the same. When Stella's smoking corpse hit the floor with a thud, Shawn was gone.

The Ladder having burnt itself out, there was heavy silence in the echo of Stella's fallen body. Mark stood over her, motionless. The dim red glow had faded, leaving the natural light of dusk flooding in from the third-floor windows outside this small room. Nate was surprised to discover just how small it was—the door, and what lay beyond it, had loomed large in the shadows of his life. But now he saw it for what it was. It was only the pain contained inside that made it seem big.

The siblings stood stunned, no one speaking until Gunther stepped into the room.

"Holy fuck," he said, moving closer to the body. "What happened?"

Nate looked at Aury. No witnesses, save themselves and Mark. This could go however they chose.

"It was the Ladder," he managed to say. "She picked up the bat, and it touched the arc. It electrocuted her."

Mark turned slowly, his expression unreadable.

"Oh, shit," said Gunther, pushing his hair back with both hands. "Oh fuck, we're in deep shit. God damn it, I told Helter not to use the fucking thing—Jesus, we're going to jail, aren't we?" He put a hand over his mouth. "Shit, I'm sorry, what an asshole—I'm worried about myself when your mom just—"

"Stella," said Katy in a deadened tone, her eyes still locked on the corpse. "She wasn't our mom. We didn't have one."

"Anyway it wasn't your fault," said Aury. "It was mine. I did all this, set it up. I'm responsible. If anyone's going to jail, it's me."

Carrie came softly into the room and stopped at Nate's side. "You're not going to jail, Aury."

"That's right," said Mark. "You didn't do this, honey." He looked at Gunther. "You won't be in any trouble, either, son. I did this. I pushed her, which means I killed her. Simple as that."

Aury turned to him with narrowed eyes. "That's not necessary."

"But is it what happened?" asked Carrie, her gaze moving between Mark and Aury.

"It *was* necessary," said Mark. "I know it wasn't what anyone meant to happen. But it needed to." He looked down at Stella's corpse again, his head hung low. "I needed to do it."

"Why?" asked Aury, fury in her voice. "You weren't part of this family. You got away from her. So why now all of a sudden do you think you need to ride in on a white horse? We needed you *then*, when we were kids. Not now."

"It's *because* I left back then that I had to come back now." He raised his gaze to hers. "I was a coward. I loved you kids, but not enough to overcome my self-interest. I've regretted it ever since. My whole life long, I've been sorry."

"Sorry doesn't cut it," said Aury coldly, and Nate flinched. Another of Stella's timeworn phrases. No matter the transgression, no matter how sincere and desperate the apology, it was never good enough. He wondered how deeply Aury was programmed. How deep they all were. How long would it be before pieces of Stella stopped seeping from their mouths and minds?

"I'm aware of that," Mark said softly. "But it's all I had."

"Are we supposed to thank you? You think you gave us some great gift?" She advanced on him, but kept her arms wrapped tightly around herself. "You took it from us. From me. I planned this so fucking carefully, do you know how long I've been waiting for this day? Years and fucking *years* of watching her, paying for all her bullshit, never living my own life. Agreeing with every shitty accusation, every nasty little gaslighting attempt. All because I wanted her exposed for what she was. I can't stand what everyone's thought about Shawn all these years. About *her*. Treating her like some damaged martyr while she soaks up the sympathy and attention. Acting like my brother's memory is dirt. And then you, you come along and fuck it up, and now how will anyone ever know?"

"We know," said Carrie. "And you've always known. All three of you."

Aury didn't seem to hear her, tears streaming down her reddened cheeks. "If I can't fix what happened that day, how will I ever fix myself? How will I ever become anything other than *this*?" She spat the last word, gesturing violently to encompass everything, every part of herself. The hatred in her voice broke Nate's heart and he went to her side.

"Aury, it's okay. It's over. Time to step back." He placed his hands on his sister's shoulders, the weight of his presence only, not making an attempt to pull her away. Fighting her wouldn't help anything—it was the only way the Lascos knew how to be, but it was time to stop struggling.

"I had a promise to keep," said Mark.

Aury stumbled back from him, her teeth clenched. "This is how you keep a promise?"

Mark looked at each of them in turn, his eyes deep wells of regret. "The promise wasn't to you, honey." He gave a sad smile, but his next words were for Carrie. "It was to her, to Stella."

Nate frowned, hating the dip of disappointment in his gut. He hadn't laid eyes on the man in decades, so why did it hurt so much to once again be looked over, to be ignored in favor of what Stella needed? "What does that mean? What promise did you make her?"

Mark kept his eyes on Carrie, making sure she was listening. "I promised her years ago, that if it ever came back, if it put you kids in danger, that I would end it. I would end *her*." He gave a shuddering sigh. "And it did come back. So I did what I said I would."

Carrie nodded, her gaze locked with Mark's. "I hear you," she said.

# THE DAY OF THE DOOR

The wail of sirens rose in the distance, and Nate pulled Aury to him, turned her to face him and wrapped her in a hug. It was awkward—none of them were good at physical affection, and it used to be a point of pride for Nate. He was a man's man finally, no need for tears or touch, a far cry from the weak boy he'd been the day his brother died. Now he let the tears run down his face without shame or regret. After a minute Katy came to join them, tucking herself beneath their arms, where she'd always been the safest. It was hot and uncomfortable, sharp elbows and scratchy sweaters everywhere he touched, but it was also the best he'd felt in decades.

"We suck at this," rasped Aury, and his grip on her tightened.

"Yeah. We'll just have to learn."

# CHAPTER TWENTY-FIVE

"**H**OW MUCH OF it was real?"

Nate's words came out easy, relaxed, unfettered by the usual constraints of social anxiety and worry. Leaning back against Carrie's couch, his arms propped on his raised knees, he felt loose in a way that usually took three scotches to achieve, but tonight his head was clear, his blood clean of that particular crutch. It had been surprisingly easy to give up, once everything was over with.

Carrie cradled a cup of hot chocolate, a ludicrous number of marshmallows bulging from the top. She raised an eyebrow. "Still having trouble with belief? Even after all of that?" She took a sip and settled back into her easy chair.

Nate looked down. "Not entirely, no. As much as I want to, I can't deny some of it was paranormal." The word felt awkward in his mouth after a lifetime of denial, but even he knew how weak his acquiescence sounded. *Some of it was paranormal.* As though the hell they'd experienced was no more than a planchette sliding across a Ouija board or a door creaking open on its own. What happened left no room for doubt, but skepticism was comfortable. He took a breath and amended his statement. "There was Shawn," he said softly. He would never deny his brother's truth again.

She nodded. "Yes, there was."

"Has that happened to you before?" he asked. "Something—*someone* manifesting to that degree? I mean it wasn't just the gizmo stuff, was it? We saw him. I *felt* him." He rubbed absently at his wrist.

208

She shrugged. "It's rare. Like I said before, hauntings are usually caused by residual emotions, not actual spirits. Even when they're sentient, they're limited in what they can do. More like those other entities we saw briefly. But given the proper motivation, sometimes they're more corporeal than others. There's a good chance the Jacob's Ladder helped."

It had certainly helped in other ways, thought Nate, but kept that to himself. "Guess we ought to thank Helter for that, huh?"

The smile fell from her face and her brows drew together, troubled. "You can try. As far as I've heard, he hasn't said a word since he was carried out of that house."

Nate's shoulders sagged, guilt creeping in. "Is he healing up?"

"Physically, yes. His right eye had to be removed, but he's regained vision in his left. The infected wounds have cleared, and they were able to graft skin from his thigh to cover the bigger missing spots on his face."

Nate swallowed a splash of bile at the thought of those gaping patches of red, the gouges along Helter's chin and jawline. It looked like something tried to pull his face right off. No, not pull, and not *someone*. He was done with denial. Stella had tried her damnedest to bite it off, and Nate would hear the sound of those clacking teeth in his nightmares the rest of his life.

"I understand they're looking at plastic surgery options, once he's better healed."

Nate looked up. "Is he . . . can he afford that? I can contribute some, if you think it'll help."

Carrie shook her head. "It's been taken care of."

"Aury?"

She shrugged. "Probably some of it. The rest from Gunther—that kid is painfully ethical, and *The Cleaners!* is making money hand over fist."

He grimaced. "I bet."

She cocked her head at him. "Have you seen it? The episode?"

"More like a mini-series."

She smiled. "There was a lot of material to get through. He did a good job editing, I thought."

"Yeah."

"How do you feel about it being out there? Not just the paranormal stuff, but all the family history?"

Nate blew out a breath. "Better than I expected to. I thought about shutting it down—I think Gunther would have handed it over if we'd asked. But keeping family secrets only ever benefited Stella. Now it's out there, getting millions of hits, which means millions of opportunities for people to know what really happened. It's what Aury wanted all along—Shawn's vindication."

Carrie nodded. "I agree. In general I avoid the comment section of any piece of media, but I made an exception, and the majority of viewers are outraged at Stella."

"Good," he said harshly. He chuckled after a moment. "Gunther's fucked, though. He'll never top it."

Carrie laughed. "True. But what a note to go out on."

Nate sighed. "Do you think . . . I mean, does that mean Shawn's been there this whole time? Haunting that shitty house by himself, alone?"

Carrie frowned. "It's unlikely. I didn't feel him there the night we went without Stella. My guess is he showed up that last time because you needed him, no other reason. And before you ask, no, I don't believe for a second he was visiting Stella. I don't know if she made that part up, or if she really was being haunted, but it wasn't Shawn."

"Was it . . . those other people? Are they all trapped there? Have they always been?"

She pursed her lips and considered, then shook her head. "I didn't feel them, either. It was more like a window opening, for a short time. All that energy—from Stella, and the machines—they saw an opportunity to slip through, so they did."

He breathed a little easier. "Then what about the fingers? You don't think Shawn did that?"

"I still think that was human agency. We noticed they were frozen, remember? And the flesh was necrotic—I took them with me, asked a doctor friend to take a look. They'd been removed from a corpse, post mortem, then frozen. Likely from a funeral home, maybe a scheduled cremation."

Nate's stomach roiled a bit and he swallowed hard. "Pretty fucking macabre. Who do you think did it?"

"Helter, if I had to guess."

Nate recoiled. "Jesus, *why*? For ratings?"

She shrugged. "If we want to be uncharitable, sure. But I suspect they were like the ionizers and the Ladder. I'm betting he rigged them on the third floor somehow, and you stepping up there triggered it. He wanted to provoke something, whether it was Stella herself or something else. And it might have worked if Stella hadn't thrown herself down the stairs as a distraction."

Nate forced a laugh. "Not sure I buy that. It's kinda Scooby Doo, isn't it? It was that pesky kid all along."

Carrie smiled. "I could be wrong."

"So that was it—parlor tricks the whole time?"

"Not the whole time, and you know it. I never found anything to explain that sound, though it's possible Gunther removed it. You saw those people, those ghosts, same as I did. And you've already said you accept Shawn's presence. So what is it you're getting at? What do you want to know?"

He sighed. "The other stuff. The other *thing*, I guess. Stella's fucking friend."

"Ah."

He kept his gaze on the floor, picking at his cuticles viciously. "I mean, it's just so fucking infuriating. Whatever the fuck Helter thought, the point of what Aury was doing, what we were *all* doing, wasn't to prove Stella right. It was to debunk her bullshit and make her take responsibility. And now she fucking wins. Buncha lights go out and some other spooky shit and presto change-o, she's not an abusive narcissistic monster anymore, just a poor little old victim of a demon or whatever."

"Is that what you believe?"

His cuticles bleeding, he forced his hands to be still. "No. I don't fucking know. There was a lot that went down at that house, and Shawn wasn't responsible for all of it. You heard the whole talk box thing—he wanted to warn us. Against what, if not some other entity? And if Shawn believed, then I'm pretty well obligated to as well, aren't I?"

"What if it wasn't an entity at all, but Stella herself he was warning about?"

Nate frowned. "What about the wind? Whatever put out those candles, made the noises. And I watched that *thing*—it was separate from Stella, and it took her over, right before she attacked Helter." His stomach turned, thinking of the condition of the kid's face when they'd found him, crouched in Katy's old closet, where something used to watch from the shadows.

"It's what we talked about, right before everything went to hell. She was capable of manipulating the physical environment all on her own. It's a common occurrence as well, often labeled poltergeist activity, but it's really a person doing it, usually the one who's the focus of everything. She could have manifested a visible shadow, but the rest, the violence, that was her."

He wanted to believe it, to believe her, but it was that want that made him reject it. Nate always had trouble with anything that gave him comfort. Always waiting for the other shoe to drop, to have that comfort yanked away. "Then why did Shawn say what he did? When I asked him if Stella killed him, he said yes, and no. So what does that mean, if all of that shit was just her?"

"I don't know. We may never know." She cocked her head at him. "Why does that bother you so much?"

"Because then it's not her fault," he said, working to keep his voice even. "It was the fucking *entity*." He hooked his fingers in air quotes.

"Let's say it was. Giving the benefit of the doubt, let's say Stella was truly, unequivocally possessed. Why do you think that absolves her of blame?"

He frowned. "Doesn't it? If she wasn't in control . . . "

"But *why* wasn't she in control?" She sat forward, her gaze intent on his.

"I don't follow."

"Let me ask you this. When you were kids, and she'd go off onto these abusive tangents—screaming and gaslighting and over-the-top punishments. Did you ever see her struggle with it? Did she ever once offer comfort after the fact, accept any blame? Apologize?"

Nate laughed harshly. "*Apologize?* You met her, right?"

Carrie smiled. "Exactly. It wasn't in her to apologize, because she was incapable of self-reflection. I'm betting that was a lifelong affliction, and didn't start just when you moved to Harper Lane."

Nate thought about it. "You're right. I can't remember her ever saying she was sorry, or admitting she was wrong. No matter how insane the circumstances, she'd rather turn her back on the truth than for one second have to admit she wasn't perfection itself."

"Everyone in this life does things they regret. Everyone loses control at one time or another. Many times there are exacerbating factors—anyone is more likely to snap when they're exhausted or stressed, for example. It's what you do about it that matters. Well-adjusted adults are capable of course correction. Their empathy allows them to see they've caused harm, and they do something about it. But Stella never did. She never fought the desire to cause harm, whether internal or instigated by something inhabiting her. She never made an attempt to get you kids out of harm's way. If the house really was haunted, if she was possessed with something that told her to hurt her children, what does that say about her?"

Nate's mouth dropped open. "I didn't . . . I never

thought of that. But that's . . . is that what you would do? If it were your kid?"

Her jaw tightened. "You're goddamn right. Parenting is a privilege, but the concept of sacrifice is baked into it." For a moment it looked like she would say more, but then she took a breath and smiled. "Think about *The Exorcist*. Chris stayed with Regan even when it put her at risk, because Regan was her child. That's a mother's job. But if the script was flipped, if Chris was the one possessed, she'd have gotten that little girl out of range the first time she realized something was wrong. She'd have fought it tooth and nail, because harming her child would be anathema."

"But what about mental illness?"

Carrie lifted her chin. "What about it?"

"Come on, this is what we do for a living. And neither of us buy into the idea that people with mental illness are to blame for not trying harder. Stella was mentally ill. There's no doubt in my mind."

"Mine, either. And you're absolutely right, people suffering from mental illness need help, not blame. But does that mean it doesn't matter who they hurt? Does it mean no one has a responsibility to protect vulnerable children from the fallout of that? Don't worry, I'm not expecting you to answer. And it's complicated, for certain. But Stella had choices, all the way along the line. She had endless opportunities to do better, to protect you kids, even if it meant leaving you in the care of your father. She never even tried."

It was true—she hadn't. Not even once, and Nate was taken aback by the wave of grief that realization brought. He'd thought he was done with that, where Stella was concerned at least. It had been many years since he'd held any hope of a sliver of maternal care as other people experienced it, so why did it hurt so much, realizing she'd never lifted a finger to protect them from herself?

"You don't have to hate her, Nate," Carrie said softly. "If you find yourself with empathy, with pity, that's okay. None of that absolves her from blame, either."

He dipped his head so she wouldn't see the revulsion that crossed his face. He didn't think he'd ever feel anything but a burning hate for the woman who birthed him. But did that make him any better? Nate had his own rage to contend with, his own shitty genetics and violent tendencies. He hadn't always controlled them, so why did he think he was exempt from judgment? No matter what happened, whatever freedoms might result from Stella's death, he'd never be safe around people.

"Nathan."

She waited until he looked up at her.

"You *do* have control. You realize that, don't you?"

He dropped his gaze again. "You don't understand. The way I felt when I . . . gave in, or whatever. I've never felt like that before."

"Angry, you mean?"

He waved an impatient hand. "Are you kidding me? I've spent half my life angry. This was something different, something more. And the worst part was I *liked* it. I usually hate being mad, it's uncomfortable as hell. But whatever was really going on, it felt . . . amazing. So what does that say about me?"

"Of course it felt good. Contrary to what you and your siblings were raised to believe, anger is a normal, healthy and helpful emotion. It's evolutionary, for fuck's sake, and it's warranted in a lot of occasions, particularly this one. What you typically describe as anger is much closer to anxiety, which is why it feels like shit. Your pulse is erratic, it gets hard to breathe, and you feel powerless. And to make matters worse, you always feel shame in its wake, don't you?"

He bit his lip and nodded slowly. "Because I should have better control than that. I'm a grown man, and I just fly off the handle all the time. You don't have to be the Hulk to be unlikable when you're angry."

She threw her head back and laughed. "I'm stealing that."

He smiled reluctantly. "It's true, though."

"In some cases, sure. But you and Aury and Katy are a product of your upbringing. I see it all the time, and not just with children of narcissists. It's a knee-jerk urge for parents to calm and end their kids' emotional outbursts. They try to stop the meltdown, be it tears or a tantrum, and a lot of times it comes from a good place. But think about that, the message it sends. All the adults get upset when the child displays a perfectly normal reaction, then they're praised when they stop. They get the idea that they're only loved as long as they're happy and calm, that anger and hurt makes them unlovable. That's where the shame comes from."

Nate blinked, feeling the truth of what she said. He'd never looked at it that way, but it made all the sense in the world. He struggled with what to say, but she spared him the necessity.

"How's Mark doing?"

He sighed. "He's okay, I guess. The lawyer Aury retained is a good one, there's a chance he won't have to serve much time. She's making a case for self-defense and defense of others."

"Have you been to visit him?"

Nate lifted a shoulder. "Once. He told me not to come back, that it wasn't necessary."

"How did he seem?"

"Okay, I guess. I don't actually know the man that well, but he seems . . . not content exactly, maybe complacent?"

Carrie nodded, silent while she finished chewing a mouthful of marshmallows. Nate regretted turning down her offer of a cup of his own.

"He probably is," she said finally. "I believed him when he said this stuff with Stella bothered him his whole life. What about Aury? Do you talk much?"

"We do, actually, much more than we used to. We get dinner once a week, all three of us. But Aury won't talk about any of the family shit—she changes the subject, says we've let it shadow our lives enough. She's finally looking to the future."

Carrie smiled. "That's a good thing, isn't it?"

"I guess. I'm still not happy with her for keeping everything from us. Shawn's exhumation, everything she learned from it. However well she meant, it was selfish."

She raised an eyebrow. "Perhaps. But haven't you done the same in the past? Kept information from your sisters to protect them?"

He pursed his lips. "Yeah, I guess so. It's how we were raised—information was currency. It got kind of ingrained, I suppose."

Carrie nodded once, then stood. "Well, then. I suggest you follow your sister's lead and find out who you are outside of Stella's orbit. Start living for the future."

He took the hint and got to his feet, stretching his lower back. "Not sure I know how to do that."

She smiled and gestured for him to precede her to the foyer. "I have faith you'll figure it out. All of you."

"Yeah. I just wish . . . " He sighed, smiled. "I guess everyone's afraid of becoming their parents, of not doing better than them."

Carrie paused with her hand on the front door, turned to look at him. "You can't control genetics, or upbringing. But she made her choices, and you make yours. Remember that, Nate."

He took a deep breath in and out, for once letting a good thing take hold, become part of his truth. He thought about kissing her on the cheek, decided against it. She was right, he had choices, free will. All at once the world looked like a bigger, brighter place, and when he went out into the frigid night, it was with a smile on his face and a weight off his shoulders.

Carrie watched him go from behind the curtains of her front room—it wouldn't do to give him any encouragement on a romantic front. He likely believed his crush was a well-kept secret, but it was hard to miss. She'd considered it, briefly. He was an attractive man, with a good heart and a drive to help others. If she had a type, he might be it, but an entanglement like that that wasn't what either of them needed, and she valued him far more as a colleague and friend.

When his glowing red taillights disappeared around a corner, she made her way slowly back to her desk and stood staring at the edge of a manila envelope imperfectly concealed beneath a magazine. She'd read the contents, prepared for her by an investigator she trusted. She didn't have the luxury of doubt, but she wasn't sure what to do about it.

There had been a history to the place, though Carrie wasn't surprised it had eluded Aury's research. A family annihilator situation, back near the turn of the last century. A father, a prominent businessman with close ties to the governor, so no wonder it had been hushed up. The extent of that cover-up was unusual, though. No names for the family, and no location for the house. It had taken every ounce of her investigator's considerable skill set to pin it down to the house on Harper Lane. Beyond that, all he'd been able to turn up had to do with the crime scene—the man found sitting in the closet of his youngest son's room, the doors half-closed, a bloody ax across his lap. Dried blood and curling flesh beneath his jagged nails, wedged between his molars. His three children and wife dead and dismembered at his hand, stacked in the third-floor room above like so much firewood. The crime scene photos in black and white haunted Carrie's mind—so much blood and pain contained in four by six representations. Dead and empty eyes, torsos with bloody stumps where limbs should be. Clawed and bloody faces, as though their murderer had tired of using the ax blade and used his fingers and teeth to get down deep. And the man's eyes . . . a strange light seemed to glow from them behind his glasses. A result of the camera flash, surely, yet it made her uneasy.

Whatever lurked at the house on Harper Lane, it hadn't left with Stella's passing, and Carrie had a feeling she hadn't seen the last of it. Whether it was the man who'd chopped his family up years before Stella moved in, or something older, she couldn't be sure. She'd give a lot to know whether Stella had been telling the truth about the history of the place, or if she'd only been spinning another lie. It wasn't an impossibility that she'd been able to uncover what Helter and Gunther hadn't, but Carrie couldn't help wondering if something had dripped the tale like poison into her fertile mind. There had been so many tormented spirits there that night, not all of them explained by what her investigator uncovered.

She felt a brief guilt for not telling Nate about it. She'd been fully prepared to offer up the report if he expressed interest, but he still fought so hard against belief. He'd keep Shawn's presence close to his heart, and everything else would fade. Besides, she *had* told him the truth. Be it supernatural agency or simply the cycle of familial abuse, Nate had control. He had choices, and she trusted that no matter what version of him looked out upon the world, he'd make the right ones.

# ACKNOWLEDGEMENTS

A million thanks go to Max and Lori Booth of Ghoulish, for trusting me once more and getting my words into the world. It's a pleasure to work with y'all, from acquisition to editing (always more em-dashes), layout, marketing, and keeping the stories alive.

Thanks to Trevor Henderson for another nightmare-inducing cover—your work is an inspiration to always up the ante in scaring the heck out of people.

To Lilyn George, for keen-eyed beta reading, and S.H. Cooper for keeping me motivated. Y'all's friendship means the world.

To James Sabata for early eyes and on-point suggestions. And for being my bestie from another teste. (Yes I stole that from you, what are you gonna do about it?)

To Jessica Clark and Stephanie Woolery, my horror girls forever. I'm lucky to have you in my life.

To Julia Ritchie, who's friendship over the last twenty years has been priceless, and who reads my work even when it's gross. Thanks for demanding I manifest.

To Young-Eun Park—you may live across the country now but you have a forever place in my heart.

To Jill Riddell, who has given so much of herself and encouraged me in every aspect.

To Christy, Joe and Quinton Lewis, for friendship, and for getting it. Love you guys.

To Anton Cancre, who has a better heart than any of us deserve.

To my co-workers of eleven years now. There's a reason I can say I love my job with a straight face, and y'all are it. Thanks for the support and the headspace.

To Ryan Lewis, for amazing representation, prescient observations, and reminding me to celebrate every milestone.

To my fellow writers, who are too numerous to name, but who keep me bolstered, sane, and excited to do what we do.

To the tireless booksellers who fight for indie horror, who make a place for us, and are a vital part of our community. You are now, and have always been, one of us.

To the reviewers and readers—you gift me with your time, a precious commodity, and I am eternally grateful. Of all the many ways to say thank you, none of them ever seem like quite enough. Without you I couldn't do what I do.

To Alan Hightower, Rachel and Wes Ballard, Isaac, Everett, and Elowen—how so many cool people ended up in one family will forever remain a mystery.

To Arthur Wells, who will always by my eldest kiddo. I'm so proud of you, every damn day.

To David, my partner in life. Thanks for learning the care and feeding of a writer.

And as always, to Sebastian. Writer or not, I've never had the words to encompass how much you bring to my life, but I hope you know anyway. You're the reason for all I do.

# ABOUT THE AUTHOR

Laurel Hightower grew up in Lexington, Kentucky, and after forays to California and Tennessee, has returned home to horse country where she lives with her husband, son, and a rescue pitbull. She's a fan of true life ghost stories, horror movies, and good bourbon. She is the Bram Stoker-nominated author of *Whispers In The Dark, Crossroads, Below, Silent Key,* and the short story collection *Every Woman Knows This,* and has more than a dozen short story credits to her name. *Crossroads* was the recipient of an Independent Audiobook Award in 2020 in the category of Best Horror, as well as the This is Horror Best Novella Award for 2020. She has also co-edited three anthologies: *We Are Wolves*, a charity anthology released in 2020 by Burial Day Press, *The Dead Inside*, an anthology of identity horror released in 2022 by Dark Dispatch, and *Shattered & Splintered*, a charity anthology released in 2022 to benefit the Glen Haven Area Volunteer Fire Department, who saved the historic Stanley Hotel from wildfires in 2020.

**Patreon:**
www.patreon.com/ghoulishbooks

**Website:**
www.Ghoulish.rip

**Facebook:**
www.facebook.com/GhoulishBooks

**Twitter:**
@GhoulishBooks

**Instagram:**
@GhoulishBookstore

**Linktree:**
linktr.ee/ghoulishbooks

Printed in the USA
CPSIA information can be obtained
at www.ICGtesting.com
CBHW030448060424
6446CB00005B/18